THE ROMAN CONSPIRACY

THE ROMAN CONSPIRACY

JACK MITCHELL

Tundra Books

Text copyright © 2005 by Jack Mitchell

Published in Canada by Tundra Books,
a division of Random House of Canada Limited,
a Penguin Random House Company

Published in the United States by Tundra Books of Northern New York,
a division of Random House of Canada Limited,
a Penguin Random House Company

Library of Congress Control Number: 2005920631

Library and Archives Canada Cataloguing in Publication

Mitchell, Jack, 1977-
The Roman conspiracy / Jack Mitchell.

ISBN 978-0-88776-713-5

1. Rome – History – Conspiracy of Catiline, 65-62 B.C. – Juvenile
Fictions.
I. Title.

PS8626.I838R64 2005   JC813'.6   C2005-900541-6

Printed in Canada

www.penguinrandomhouse.ca

3 4 5 6   19 18 17 16 15

for
James R. Mitchell
my father

Characters

Spurinna	(Aulus Lucinus Spurinna) The Narrator
Hercna	Aunt of Aulus Lucinus Spurinna
Manlius	Leader of old soldiers in Etruria
Homer	Greek slave, originally from Athens and secretary to Spurinna
Volturcius	Landowner from Faesulae in Etruria, lives in Rome
Caesar	(Julius Caesar) Up-and-coming politician in Rome
Cicero	(Marcus Tullius Cicero) One of Rome's two Consuls, Protector of Spurinna family
Tullia	Daughter of Cicero
Fulvia	Friend of Tullia
The Druid	(Brennus) One of the ambassadors of the Allobroges
Pantolemos	Hired philosopher at house of Volturcius
Catiline	Roman politician, leader of a conspiracy against the Senate
Flaccus	Brave young Tribune, leader of a troop of Roman cavalry
Pomptinus	Irresponsible young Tribune, with Flaccus, leader of a troop of Roman cavalry
Antonius	One of Rome's two Consuls, commander of Roman army

Contents

Death at Dusk

"**A**ulus, there is no question of your going to Rome. You have not finished your studies."

That was my Aunt Hercna's voice. It was also her straightforward style. She was pacing up and down the room (well, not *pacing* – no Roman lady would ever *pace*, but the closest thing to it) and frowning at me. But she was also running out of excuses.

"The harvest has hardly begun. It's five days' ride, and who will go with you? I cannot spare the supervisor, not with all these troubles. And think of how expensive it is in the city. Everyone says so. And your uncle is sick, think of him here without you, and . . . and you haven't finished your studies!"

Her problem was that these were all the reasons why I *had* to go. If I did not, if no one went, the harvest, the land, my studies, my uncle's well-being – suddenly they were all threatened. But it was not my place to point that out again.

My aunt was torn. Maybe she thought I only wanted to see the gladiators at the Circus.

And just maybe, on that afternoon, she thought correctly.

The "troubles" on our land had been growing for about a year, though I had been off at school in the town, Faesulae, and I hadn't paid much attention. First there had been complaints from our tenant farmers, saying that crops were disappearing from their fields. They thought there might be an evil spirit. But my Aunt Hercna (who handled all the management of our land) found out that it was the old soldiers from the hill farms who were responsible for taking the best pumpkins and lettuce from our people. She caught one of the thieves and punished him. After that, in June, there was some real violence between the old soldiers and our farmers. Threats were traded back and forth and the hall of our house was full of worried tenants almost every day. Even though their new enemies had wrinkles and gray hair, the tenants said, the fact was, these old soldiers had discipline, and they had a leader too, named Manlius. In July, the soldiers had killed one of the bolder tenants, when he tried to stand up to them.

It had to stop, the tenants said. Who knew how far this Manlius would go? Why wasn't my uncle doing anything to stop him? He was their Protector; he had influence in Rome; couldn't he stop it, somehow? What good was a Protector who didn't help the little man? We, in turn, had our own Protector in Rome. Why, the tenants asked, didn't he help us help them? That was what a Protector was for, they said, to stand up in court and make the speech that tenants couldn't make and to pray to the gods the right way, so they would listen. To trade a favor with another powerful Protector. To uphold the Law. At least, to do *something*.

Now it was nearly November, and the old soldiers were making matters worse. Even my uncle was worse. His illness had left him in bed most of that year, and now he was asleep most days and in pain when he was awake. He couldn't deal with the old soldiers, or negotiate, or even write to his friends in the city. His Greek secretary wrote the letters and he signed them, but no answer ever came. Between Romans, business of this sort was done face to face, not with ink and wax.

Things might have continued like this, and I might never have gone to Rome or found myself arguing with my aunt that day, if Manlius had not appeared that very morning at our house. He had men with him, and the men had weapons. He had a red blotch on his neck that bloomed each time he spoke angrily, which was all the time.

"Come now," Manlius began, throwing back his cloak after the barest formalities. "Come now, it can't be that we don't understand one another. We're as many as you on the slopes, pulling our plows in the rocks, and uphill too. So there's something to be said for sharing, don't you think? Sharing out the good land?"

Manlius stood in the middle of our hall, next to the marble statue of my grandfather. He planted his hands on his hips, glaring round, looking first at his followers and then at us. Despite his farmer's cloak, he was every inch the grim old sergeant. He wore his years of army life well, and his voice still had the ring of command, even as he tried to speak politely. I stood facing him, six inches shorter and not yet wearing a grown man's toga, just my boy's striped one. Aunt Hercna sat in a chair beside me and wore a veil. My uncle was asleep. Officially, Manlius addressed me, but he knew full well that he was really speaking to my aunt. She was in charge, and she too had a will of iron.

Aunt Hercna indicated the swords our visitors were wearing, and I said, "Are you farming with your blades? Plows would do better."

Manlius scowled at me. "These instruments aren't rusty like our plows, and we don't scrape them on stony fields, I can tell you. It was these we used to get our allotments, out in the East with the General, and by the good gods, you know as well as I that we can use them again to get new allotments." He was referring to the old General, now gone, who had given the soldiers farms in our valley, back in my father's day. The land was their reward for being in his army out in Asia. Now they were threatening to take "new allotments" — our Tenants' farms, which it was our duty to defend.

"You've seen the documents. Those lands aren't yours," I answered, once my aunt had whispered to me.

"This dear lady is handy with a pen, like the Greek here," replied Manlius, looking to my uncle's secretary, "and no doubt when the time comes they'll both be handy for writing new documents for us. That'll make it quite official," he said, laughing. "What use there will be for you and your tongue, we'll have to see."

My aunt could not let this pass. "What do you mean? Will you attack us?" she cried, breaking her silence. "No rebel can last long against the Roman Law, you fool. And the law in this valley is in the hands of the Spurinnas," she added, meaning our family, "and our own Protector lives in Rome."

"I'm a fool, am I?" shouted Manlius. "Well, here's more foolishness for you! You're not the only one with friends in the city, and our friends don't wait for law courts and judges. If you won't share, we'll start sharing you out among ourselves – the whole lot of you, these farms, this house, these fields – and we could use some slaves! No, by Hercules, you won't recognize this valley in six months!" he finished. He tried to laugh, though he was far too worked up to manage it. The blotch on his neck glowed as red as fire.

With that, and one last insult from Manlius that we "didn't even have a man in the house, just some child with a boy's striped toga," the morning interview ended, and the old soldiers had left with more sneers and insults. I could not see how it could have gone worse. But my aunt was satisfied, even proud of me.

"You did rightly, Aulus, answering as well as he did. We have no choice. At least the farmers will not say the Spurinnas gave them up because they were afraid of a gang of highway robbers!"

Obviously, my aunt still hoped the letters from my uncle would reach our Protector in the city. Cicero was his name, and he was a very influential man, one of Rome's two Consuls. He had known my father, Aunt Hercna said, and he wouldn't forget our family, even if he was also a very busy man. I had my doubts, and I voiced them at the sixth hour, when we ate lunch.

"Why not send me instead of writing?" I asked. "I know the facts, and I'll convince him. They say I look like father, and maybe that will help. Cicero can send his men to deal with Manlius."

The idea of my going didn't sit well with my aunt, however. Even though she was a stern woman when it came to business and running our land, she found my presence reassuring. I might be dressed like a boy, but while I was there she had at least one ally. So we argued for an hour, until she repeated with great authority, "Aulus, there is no question of your going to Rome. You have not finished your studies."

With that I was sent off to continue those studies. I had come home from Faesulae to help with the harvest, but the feud with Manlius had thrown all that into confusion, so instead of directing the slaves in the fields, I was studying in my room. But it was Greek grammar and somehow, after the first wrangle with Manlius and the second with Aunt Hercna, I couldn't concentrate. So I slipped down the back stairs to the cabbage field. It was my favorite spot for my favorite sport – throwing the javelin.

I had a straw dummy there, propped against the trunk of the oak tree, as a target. The dummy and the special set of three javelin-heads had been a joint birthday present from the groom and the blacksmith, old slaves from my father's time. I had shaped the wooden javelin shafts myself – that was my end of the bargain – and, after eight months of practice, my grip, my throwing motion, and my follow-through (the important part) were so natural I didn't even think about them any more. I just picked a point on the target dummy and – *thunk* – usually came pretty close, from thirty yards. By Hercules, looking at my right shoulder – *thunk* – you could tell it was bigger than the left one, much stronger. One for the chest now – *thunk* – and spot on target, quite good! Then the inevitable walk to pick up the javelins, hanging limply from the dummy. And then to begin again. Normally it was relaxing; but this time I threw the shafts quick and fast, for I was imagining Manlius' ugly face there on the straw dummy.

"If it comes to a fight," I thought, "I could get him, right in front of the house, and that might turn the tide in the battle."

By the time it was dusk and almost the hour for the supper bell, I began to feel sore. Just as I was walking up to the trunk for the fiftieth time, I froze in my tracks. Someone was screaming in the house, a high-pitched woman's scream. Before I could move, it pierced the air again, this time accompanied by the sobbing voices of many women. They were howling, shrieking with grief. I felt like I'd been kicked in the stomach.

Homer, my uncle's Greek secretary, came scrambling round the house, calling out my name. "Master Aulus, sir! Where are you? Young master!" He trampled through the cabbages and came straight for me as best he could (he was not very athletic). I had never seen him with such an expression of incomprehension on his face. "Master Aulus," he panted, "Your uncle – sir, your uncle is dead."

I Take the Road to Rome

When the funeral pyre was cold, the slaves gloomily gathered my uncle's ashes. My aunt placed the urn in the tomb of his ancestors, beside his brother's – my father's. The soothsayer pronounced some phrases in the old tongue, Etruscan. "*Ikan netsuis alpnu Cnevus aplus turuce,*" he intoned. He was the only one who understood. The rest of us only spoke Latin, the modern language.

My aunt and I were dressed in white, for mourning, and our eyes were red. It had been a terrible night. I had not slept much. Gray clouds covered the sky. The air seemed to weigh heavily on us as we trudged slowly back to the house along a lane of dark cypress, with our tenants in procession.

The funeral wasn't the last ceremony that day, however. My uncle's death left me as the only male member of the family – the heir – and my aunt and Homer, after a quick glance at the accounting records, told me it was essential that I inherit the family property without delay. So right after the funeral I had to go through the coming-of-age

9

ceremony – out of season, and rather before I'd planned to. I was supposed to have waited for the manhood festival next Spring. My voice was already breaking, though, to some extent.

There was something exhilarating about wrapping the full, plain, unornamented toga around myself, leaving the boy's striped garment behind forever. Suddenly it was my job to pour the offering in front of the family shrine, standing where my uncle had always stood. And the tenants, who were on hand as witnesses, hailed me in the hall as "Aulus Lucinus Spurinna, keeper of the peace, Protector of the valley, upholder of the law." Some of them looked skeptical, but most seemed glad to intone those words. I had the same name as my grandfather, Aulus Lucinus Spurinna, and his days were remembered as peaceful and prosperous times.

Officially, I was now a man; secretly I felt younger than ever before.

My uneasiness through all these rituals, gestures, and formalities was increased by the fact that Homer, the Greek secretary, kept fidgeting the whole time, even when I was performing the offering at the shrine. He even tried to speak once, which was absolutely forbidden during the ceremony, especially for slaves, but my aunt caught him and gave him a withering look that closed his mouth like a trap. After that he confined himself to trying to signal me urgently with his hands. I ignored him. No doubt there was important administrative work to deal with, but wasn't that his job? After I had greeted all the tenants, wished them well, and bade them farewell, I had to receive the pledge of loyalty from each of the household slaves – cook, groom, maids, blacksmith, gardener, swineherd, and all the rest. And there was Homer, last in the line, and looking very anxious.

"Sir, if I could have a word with you . . ."

"Aren't you going to pledge me your loyalty too?" I asked.

"Oh, right! Yes, sir! Yes. And if I could add to that by just showing you . . ."

I turned away. He and Aunt Hercna had already put me through two grueling ceremonies that day, and I wasn't ready for a third. No doubt Homer wanted me to approve next month's wine shipment or something.

I went out the back door, still in my new toga, and walked away from the house. The smell of bleach was still strong in the white wool that covered me, but as I went up the hill path the familiar scent of the pine trees replaced it. It was hard to believe how much had happened in one day. But I looked over our land and felt happy, then melancholy, and then happy again, all in an instant. I loved the familiar vista of the farmers' cottages and their high, full crops; of the creek wending its way past the tall pillars and high roof of our house; of the evening rumble of wheels on the distant road; of the remote range of hills, the hills of home whose outlines were etched in my memory. I was sad to be leaving, and yet happy again, for at last I was going – I didn't know where. To Rome of course, but who knew where else?

Yes, I had decided to take the road to Rome. Now that I was head of the family, my aunt couldn't prevent me. I had decided to fight for our land. Not with the javelin, as I'd thought. There was no stopping soldiers with that, not when they came to steal our food, enslave the tenants, take the tenants' wives, and burn our house. Manlius would certainly be back, and soon enough, inventing an empty reason to destroy us. I almost cried out in anger to think of Aunt Hercna left to beg from door to door – could that happen? And what would happen to me, last of the Spurinnas? Obviously, they would see to it that I joined my father and my uncle.

No, the tenants might have thought it was just tradition when they hailed me as "upholder of the law," but I was serious. I would do it. I would take the case to our Protector, and then I would make Manlius eat his words. In the morning, I would ride to Rome.

Aunt Hercna looked different when she saw me and Homer off at dawn the next morning. Homer had volunteered to go with me, and since he knew more about my uncle's politics than anyone, I had no objection. Aunt Hercna gave me some silver coins; but when she kissed me goodbye, I barely felt it. She had been weeping again. Perhaps she was just too sad to try and stop me. We mounted our beasts, the white mare for me and the donkey for Homer, waving 'til the path from the house turned a corner at the well and began to run down to the Roman highway.

For the first few miles we rode in silence. Homer seemed less eager to talk, confident perhaps that the five days of travel would leave him plenty of time for discussions. My uncle had bought Homer in Athens a dozen years ago, and he'd been his secretary ever since. Although he must have felt my uncle's death as keenly as my aunt, he whistled a Greek tune as the sun rose high. His saddlebags were bursting with documents and letters, scrolls, wax tablets and ink, and a writing plume. All this apparatus jostled and rustled as the donkey trotted.

Presently we joined the Cassian Road, the old Roman stone road that cut straight and true through the hills, and we turned south. The town of Faesulae rose now on the slope to our left, but my school was invisible in the mass of red roof tiles. I was glad to be out riding beneath the bright sky, instead of sitting inside with my teacher, but I felt slightly sick to think that Manlius was the reason for my freedom. And before long the silence of the morning, Homer's whistling, and the documents' rattling got to me.

"Homer," I asked, "what on earth is that poor donkey carrying? The entire archive?"

"Just some useful proof for your Protector to look at, sir," he answered, smiling. Then he looked serious. "As well as something that you should see as soon as possible."

"And that is what?"

"You mean, what is it you should see as soon as possible, sir?"

"Yes. Stop beating about the bush, Homer!"

"Well, sir, I don't wish to bother you with paperwork, but . . ." He fished around in the saddlebag and produced a letter with a broken seal.

"A letter to my uncle?" I asked.

"No, sir, *from* your uncle." Homer passed it to me. "I wrote it myself, sir, to Cicero, your Protector. Look, this is my handwriting. This is your uncle's signature. It lays out some particulars of your dispute, together with an account of Manlius' activities in the area."

"Harassing the tenants, you mean?"

"Well, that too, sir, but much more than that. It describes the encampment they've made, together with . . ."

"What encampment?"

"If you'll just look over to your right, sir, as we cross the bridge up here," he began. I squinted over the valley of the Arrus River below us, and could see there was a sizeable wooden wall there, with a tower. I caught the glint of metal.

"It looks like an army camp!" I cried. "Are you telling me that's Manlius' work, meant for us?"

"No, sir, I believe his plans are rather bigger than just your valley. He's been up and down the whole area, collecting old soldiers. But I haven't told you how I got this letter."

"Didn't you ever send it? But the seal is broken."

"Indeed, sir. And I picked it up next to your dear uncle's bed, when they found him dead. We had sent it to Cicero, and there it was back again, and, furthermore, if you'll just notice the stains on the left-hand margin . . ."

I saw what he meant. There were bright blue marks on the papyrus sheet, as though some thick liquid had been smudged there by a finger or a thumb.

"This doesn't look like wine, or ink, or . . ." I swallowed, ". . . blood."

"Sir, I'm afraid there is only one thing it can be. Only one admixture can produce that lurid blue. It is murex and concentrated silphium, sir. One of the strongest dyes, and a deadly poison."

That was the word I had hoped he would not utter. "This means," I said weakly, "that my uncle was poisoned? But how could we not have noticed?"

Homer bit his lip. "He was so sick, sir, and though I tried to inform your aunt, she was so upset that she paid no attention."

"We must find the person who did this, Homer. We must avenge my uncle!" I cried. "But what about the tenants and the land?" I felt lost. I had been glad to have a straightforward task in going to Rome, but now I felt we should turn back and deal with this new problem. "Homer, why didn't you tell me this before?"

"With respect, sir, I did try. But look at it this way. The letter concerned Manlius and his soldiers – how he is gathering them far and wide, sir – and it seems the man who killed your uncle must have dropped it by him when he killed him. Therefore there is a link between the old soldiers and the killer. And I have a good notion who that killer is."

"What?" I exclaimed. "Homer, you know who it is?"

"Well, not for certain, sir, no. But I think it was the man who used to take your uncle's letters, including this one, to Rome. He owns property in Faesulae, and is in the town often. He pledged to deliver letters to your Protector in the city. Perhaps he has some connection with Manlius that we don't know, sir. Whoever it was, he intercepted the letters about Manlius."

I considered this. "And what is this man's name?"

"Volturcius, sir, a Roman knight. A small, shy man – or so I would have said from the way he behaved with your uncle. Until this," Homer shuddered. "'*An evil neighbor is a woeful curse*,' as the poet says."

"The poet?"

"Yes, sir, Hesiod, the prince of poets."

"What do you mean? You say Volturcius lives in Rome?"

"Yes, sir, though I don't know where. I never saw much of him. He always met with your uncle privately. But I would know him if I saw him."

There was a hard glint in Homer's eye. As for me, I was shocked and furious that it might have been murder that set my uncle on the pyre. But it was a relief, too, that both missions were now leading us to the same destination – Rome. I put the letter carefully into the large wallet I carried in the pouch of my toga.

"Well, thank you for telling me all this, Homer. I appreciate it. I realize you must be just as angry as I am."

Homer did not look particularly angry, however. Homer's face rarely showed much emotion. There was a Greek detachment there that rarely left him. I had seen him troubled and confused only once, when my uncle died.

By the end of our first day on the road, we reached Arretium, a small town that until now had marked the edge of our country, and so of the world – at least in my mind. My aunt had a cousin there who was happy to put us up, a learned and silver-haired gentleman with a cool Etruscan air. From Arretium we passed down the wide river valley, bordered by tall mountains topped with shadowy pines. The next two nights we spent camped on the road in the chilly night air.

On the fourth day, however, as we approached the great expanse of Lake Volsinium, which divides Etruria from the great vale of Rome, the sky began to grow a darker gray. In the afternoon it rained hard as we traveled through a wild and uninhabited stretch of country. We pushed on for some time, for I refused to waste a moment until we found this man, Volturcius, but the rain did not let up. At length we took refuge under a low tree, though this gave little shelter. Homer offered to hold his cloak over me to keep me dry, but I informed him that my first act as a full Roman man would not be to hide from rain under a Greek slave's cloak.

"I am quite of your view, sir," he said, rising and looking out from our refuge beneath the tree. "It is most philosophical. To wish to avoid what cannot be avoided – that is as foolish as to desire to have what one cannot have. Hesiod says it well, don't you think? '*The gods take note of those whose judgment errs.*'"

"He does indeed," I said, getting quite wet now, and not for the life of me grasping Homer's point.

"It is like with this rain, sir," he said. "When it rains, we get wet." And with that he stepped out from under the tree into the highway, standing there in the rain with a small smile. "Here I am now, getting wet, just as you are doing under the tree!"

"I don't see how it's so hilarious, Homer."

"You might, sir, if you weren't busy trying *not* to get wet," he said.

Besides helping Homer illustrate his philosophical points, however, the rain meant we could not go far that day. Once it subsided to a drizzling mist, we walked our beasts over the next rise. From there we made for a chimney of smoke we could barely discern about two miles ahead.

It proved to be coming from a wretched little inn; but to our eyes this was a very welcome promise of a fire and some hot soup or food. There was a painted sign at the front showing a leopard snarling in what might have been the Arena. Few people were inside, just two of the usual traveling sort on the dirty benches by the fire, a peddler and a tinker, and one drunk farmer sleeping in a corner. Not a promising sight, but the fire looked warm enough, and a girl was stirring a cauldron of soup. I sent Homer round to the stables with the horse and donkey, paid for a room, ordered us some soup to be sent to the room, and settled down to a cup of hot wine.

"Rough weather for a gentleman on the road, isn't it?" asked a strange voice.

I looked to my left and realized I had not seen the fourth man in the room sitting behind one of the wooden pillars. He was older than I was, perhaps twenty, but dressed much the same: a white toga and a wet cloak. He was unshaven, however, and I got the idea he'd been drinking as much as the sleeping farmer, but perhaps had more practice.

"I'm glad to come in for the fire," I said.

"And the wine!" he called, indicating he would like more. I told the girl to add it to my bill. "So you've got money, I see," the young man said. "Good thing – a gentleman always needs money. What's life without it, I ask you? I'll tell you. No girls, no gambling, no food, and a roof like this over your head!" He laughed derisively at the roof of the establishment. "Not much better than death, don't you think?"

"Well . . ." I began, taken aback by the fellow's intensity and his bloodshot eyes.

"I'll tell you another thing, my friend. I used to have money. A big name, I used to have, among some people in the city, and not the worst set, not by a long way's. But the marriage fell through, don't you see, and then the money-lenders started coming after me. I borrowed money, sure I did. But who's a gentleman who doesn't live a bit beyond the strict limit, after all! Look at Caesar there, borrowing left and right – and does anyone mind? Well, they might, but they don't dare say it. And they're right about that."

"Julius Caesar?" I asked. I had heard the name somewhere.

"Right, him . . . and Catiline. They're both Senators, and they know what it is to be a gentleman and have the moneylenders after you. Some people don't care. Take that Cicero, now. He's Consul, you know, though no reason he should be – look where he's from! – and he doesn't care about us younger gentlemen. There's going to be trouble, mark my words. That Catiline, he may be a tricky character, but he knows it takes money to live the good life!"

With that he downed an immense gulp of his wine and started on the cup I'd bought him. I looked over to the door for Homer, but he was taking his time. Not the best man with horses, of course.

"You mark my words, there's going to be fighting," the young man went on, now quite drunk. "If the Senate goes on listening to Cicero and doesn't care what our friend Catiline thinks, as they've *been* doing, well, we'll take matters into our own hands! If they won't lend us the money we need to be gentlemen, we'll take it! What are we, slaves? Scum? A gentleman can't stand for it, the way it is. Just as good to be born poor as to be born rich, these days. And that means trouble, for Italy, and for Cicero, and for Rome! Catiline'll see to that! You'll see flames, my friend, you'll see flames! I notice you're not drinking your wine," he added, after he took another swig.

"No, no. I think I'll go have the soup in my room. Thank you for the conversation, however," I said, and rose to go.

He insisted on embracing me, and remarked that we young people had to stick together. I made a hasty retreat to the back of the inn. It wasn't much more than a stable for people, with walls, I realized. And I found our door was locked.

The girl saw me at the door and said, "Oh, I gave the key to your slave, Hesiod was it?"

"Homer. Though he may have quoted Hesiod."

"Whatever, I gave the key to him."

I walked around to the stables, but Homer wasn't there. My mare and the donkey were well looked after, though wet. As I was patting the mare down to dry her off (since Homer had not thought to do this), I felt a strange lightness in my toga pouch. My hand shot to my belly – the wallet was gone! The large wallet where I'd put the letter with the blue stain and all my silver!

Doubling back to the door to our room, I scanned the ground. Perhaps it had dropped out there. But no luck. My heart sank.

Just then Homer appeared, carrying a tray of bowls and laughing with the girl from the inn.

"Oh, there you are, master! I had to run an errand for this rude gentleman who was leaving. He must have mistaken me for the stableboy – *me*, sir, if you can believe that – and he told me to take all his things out to his horse, a great pile of rags, while he had more wine. I'm not sure a man should ride with that much wine in him, sir, but I did as he said . . . to help Secunda here," he said, with a smile at the girl.

"Homer, Homer, has he gone? The drunk man who was here? I think . . ." I trailed off. I didn't know how to break the news.

"He's gone, sir. And good riddance, if I may add, because you'll never believe what I found in the rags as I dropped them by his horse. At first I thought he must have a wallet just like yours, but then I realized there must have been some mistake." And here he put down the soup tray, felt inside his shirt, and pulled out my wallet. With my heart in my mouth, I checked it. The letter was intact, and all the silver coins were still there.

"Homer," I cried, "I would never have taken you for a pickpocket, even as a pickpocket of other pickpockets."

"Sir," he answered, "it is as Hesiod says: '*Arrogance never helped a desperate man.*'"

"It is indeed," I observed, as the girl let us into the room. I sat down to enjoy the soup, wondering if Homer was quite as impractical a fellow as I'd thought.

The Consul's Daughter

We had fair weather the next morning; the heat was offset by wind, blowing against us as we came down from the hills. Many small rivers flowed down to our right, toward what I had never seen – the great sea that lies at the center of the world. We went down to Sutrium, on the Cassian Road, and then south from there, staying at Calepodius the fifth night, not far from Rome.

Etruria was behind us. The food was different here, the air was hotter, and people spoke more quickly, pronouncing their Latin (as it seemed to me) through their noses. We could sense the city was very close, even before we saw it.

On the morning of the sixth day, we set off before dawn and crossed the Tiber, the river of Rome, at daybreak. That is, we started over the bridge at that hour, but it took us forever to get across. There was already a huge throng of pedestrians bustling across to the Roman Market and the Cattle Market, some carrying chickens, some leading pigs, and some just stopping to chat with each other. The confusion was overwhelming. It was my first taste of the chaos that is a central street in Rome. We had to lead the beasts on foot.

"I'm sure . . . I'm sure it will be quicker on the other side," I called out to Homer, as he tried to navigate his donkey through a large family.

The thing was, we were desperate to get to my Protector's house before the sun was very high. In the country you can visit a Protector any time before noon. Everyone knows there are cows to be milked and sheep to be led out to pasture. But in the city, as Aunt Hercna had often told me, there are no errands more important than calling on your Protector first thing in the morning. And that 'first thing' was slipping by before we reached the far side of the bridge. It was maddening!

Nor was it any better on the other side. It was easy to ask directions. Cicero lived on the slope of one of the main hills, the Palatine, on Glassmakers' Street, someone said – but our first wrong turn taught us that we had to stick to the main streets and not get caught up in the labyrinth of alleys and passageways between buildings. Those main streets were a nightmare, though, for anyone in a hurry, as we were. The press of pedestrians, the sheer weight of bodies behind us, made us feel like we were caught in the pull of a brisk, narrow river. It was all I could do to cling to my mare and hope the current would eventually drop me.

On top of it all, I was making an enormous effort not to look too awed by the sheer scale of the city. We passed several buildings that were four stories tall, and try as I might I couldn't help gaping up at them. I almost walked over people when I did so, for it seemed that many people slept in the streets and stayed there all day, though what with the rain of two days before the streets themselves were as muddy as the pig pen at home.

We were not making good progress, and the thought of reaching the Protector's house too late to see him made me boil with frustration. We had nowhere to stay in the city, and I dreaded a refusal at the door and a humiliating walk back home.

At a square, not far from the Roman Market, I paused to let Homer catch up, but he must have passed me somehow, for I heard his voice over to my left.

"Homer, I'm so glad I found you!"

"Yes, sir, but you'll never believe . . ." He was out of breath, and very excited. He put his donkey's reins in my hand. "Master, you won't believe it," he continued, "but over there by the fountain, I just saw him, the Roman knight, Volturcius! He was talking to three men under the awning of the wine stall. Just now, sir!"

"Volturcius?" I exclaimed. "Are you sure, Homer? What are the odds that . . . you're sure it wasn't just a man who looked like him? Everybody's wearing a toga here."

"Almost sure, sir. Almost absolutely sure it was him!"

I was paralyzed by indecision. Yes, we had come to find the murderer, or at least find out how a man with poison had got his hands on my uncle's letter; but we also had to ask for help from Cicero, our Protector. How could we do both at the same time?

"With respect, sir," Homer volunteered, "why don't you continue to your Protector's house and I'll see if I can't find Volturcius? I can meet you at Cicero's later, and I'll even find us a place to stay."

He made it sound like a bargain. It didn't really seem like a good idea to split up, but it was the only plan on offer, so I agreed. "Look for me at Cicero's, then, but if you don't see me, come find me here in this square, alright? I'll sit by the fountain, all day if I have to."

I gave him some of the silver and he darted off like a hound on the scent, leaving me with the mare *and* his donkey. A pretty sight for a gentleman showing up unannounced on his Protector's doorstep, without even a slave to hold the beasts!

Nevertheless, I set my teeth and trudged on. It wasn't far now. I got new directions, found Glassmakers' Street, and followed it high up the hill 'til it left the apartment blocks behind. It seemed marvelously quiet after the bustle on the streets below, and I felt a gentle breeze.

Here it was: a long, smoothly plastered blank front wall, right up against the street, with a trim of painted vines in the conservative style. Apart from the fact that the wall and the street were spotless, the only signs that this was indeed the right house were the two men with long-handled axes in front of the tall iron doors. I tied the two beasts to a tree opposite the door, rearranged my toga, and walked up to them.

"My name is Aulus Lucinus Spurinna. I have come to visit my friend, Marcus Tullius Cicero. Is this his house?"

The two ax-men looked at me with amazement. Eventually one of them laughed and said, "Deliveries go round the back."

I stood my ground, pausing long enough to restore my dignity. "Do they?" I asked. "But visitors like myself enter by the front door?"

"Look, my lad, you don't understand. This is the *Consul's* house."

"Which Consul?" I asked. "Because if this is the house of Antonius, the other Consul of this year, I've lost my way. I am looking for the house of Marcus Tullius, who is the Consul and my Protector. My name is Aulus Lucinus, from Etruria."

They paused, clearly trying to decide if I was crazy or very important – or both. At last one of them reached out and hammered on the door. A steward's head appeared at once and, showing similar amazement, he asked me to come inside.

It seemed very dark in the house after the strong outdoor sun, and my eyes adjusted slowly. I was standing in a large entrance hall, twice as large as ours at home, with pictures in the modern style across the walls, busts in their niches, and very high ceilings propped on double rows of pillars. It was pleasantly cool, and quite silent. A wide fishpond lay in the open sun beyond the hall, with deeper shade behind it.

I made my bow to the house shrine and turned to the steward. I repeated my name boldly, but he was not so easily impressed as the guards. In fact, with some skepticism, he began to ask me my business. "It is far past morning, far past. Why weren't you here this morning?" he asked. I had to repeat myself, which was irritating, and I may have announced '*I have just ridden in from Etruria*' a bit more loudly than I meant to, and we might have raised our voices – he with righteous indignation – but our exchange was cut short by the sound of women's laughter and the approach of footsteps from the shadows behind the fishpond.

I looked up and saw a girl stepping briskly towards us. She was about my height and seemed about the same age, with raven-dark hair, large eyes, and a small mouth. She was wearing a light blue dress, with a veil now spread across her shoulders and down her arms. I had a feeling I was about to be thrown out.

"Now then, master steward, what is this? Shouldn't you save your strength for the party?" she called in a clear voice. As she reached him I heard her mutter, "How often do you have to hear, steward, that this is a *political* building?" But then she turned to me and inclined her head.

"Welcome, sir. I gather you know you are at Cicero's house? I am his daughter, called Tullia." And then, with the faintest eagerness: "Did I hear that correctly? You have just come to us from Etruria?"

I said yes, that I urgently needed her father's advice, that we had terrible troubles, that we had unfortunately been delayed . . .

"I am sorry you have troubles," she said sympathetically, "but you would not have seen him this morning anyway. He has been at Praeneste these last few days. He will be back tonight. Tomorrow is his speech to the Senate. I would love to learn more about your situation. We are very keen to have news from your region, but I'm terribly busy with this organizing. Perhaps you can come to the party tonight? It starts in . . ." she glanced at the sun ". . . by Hercules, in just four hours! Will you stay 'til then? I am not much company."

"That would be wonderful!" I said. "I don't mind waiting."

"Let me get you something to read. Do you want someone to read to you, or will you read yourself?"

"I can manage, I think."

"Just like me," Tullia said, smiling. "Let me show you the library."

"Library?"

"Yes, here it is." She led me up some steps. "Do you like it? It's my favorite room."

I followed her in and caught my breath. A large room, absolutely stuffed with scrolls! There must have been a thousand, each neatly labeled in its slot, many glinting with gold knobs. I was speechless: I had never seen more than fifty in one place.

"They say it's the largest Rome has ever known," she said with some satisfaction. "My father has been collecting for years. Any preferences? Latin or Greek? Or Etruscan?" she asked mischievously, referring to our old language. I settled for a biography of an old Roman hero.

"Politics! That's the style. I like you already," Tullia said, and stepped out.

Homer's Secret

The scroll kept me busy for about an hour, but by the time the hero of the tale was receiving the warm thanks of the Senate and the Roman People, I was having trouble paying attention. Not that it was hard to read: it was written in a clean, patient hand, with wide margins on smooth papyrus; but I was so full of excitement and nervous energy that I soon found myself lying on the couch with the bookroll in my hand, looking at the inlaid ceiling.

Anything, good or bad, seemed possible. I pictured Cicero greeting me with joy and promising immediate assistance. Or laughing at how young I was, how unworthy of help. Or blandly refusing to get involved. Or somehow noticing I was a boy who never learned his Greek grammar very well in school. I must have fallen asleep, because the next thing I knew the steward was at the door, hoping I was well, and adding that it was the ninth hour since dawn and my presence was cordially requested at the dinner party.

"The party, of course," I said, standing up and rearranging my toga.

He led me back downstairs, but not to the hall this time. The guests were gathering in the private garden at the back. It was a shady, spacious spot, with a wide, round pool in which gleaming red and green fish darted to and fro. There was a heavy scent of thyme, and soft music was just audible in the background of many conversations. There must have been fifty people there, young and old. The women's gowns were of every possible color, while on many of the men's white togas there blazed the single purple stripe of a Senator. And to think I had been so proud of my simple toga of manhood!

Tullia saw me standing on the edge of the crowd and called out. She was sitting on one of the marble benches with two of her friends, and I hurried over, trying not to step on any Senators' togas.

"Spurinna!" she said. "Here you are at last. I must choose you a less interesting tale to read next time. I have just been describing your encounter with the steward in the hall. May I introduce you? Here is Marrucinus, and this is my best friend, Fulvia."

I bowed to them both, embarrassed that my encounter with the steward should be my introduction, but Marrucinus

smiled sympathetically and Fulvia just raised her eyebrows at me and said, "So the steward strikes again." Not
to be outdone, Marrucinus coughed and tried to put it
into verse:

"Hell's guardian dog will never have looked drearier
Than when he finds your steward's his superior."

We laughed, except for Fulvia who was instantly ready to
follow up with her own couplet, but Tullia cut her off.

"No more verse, Fulvia, or we'll never get to . . . Wait a
second! Marrucinus, were you just comparing my house to
hell? By implication?"

Fortunately for Marrucinus, just then the music
stopped and the note of a horn announced dinner. Our
group dissolved, for Fulvia was seated at a different table
from ours, it seemed, and for a moment I was terrified
that Tullia wouldn't be at mine – there were five tables.
But a slave took my elbow and showed me to my place
at a small table in the far corner of the large and (to my
eyes) luxurious dining hall. Tullia lay down at the same
one, just to my left.

There were only two guests to a side, which gave us six
places – the side facing the center of the room was left open
for the waiters bringing food. I spread my napkin in front
of me on the couch and washed my fingers when the waiter

brought the bowl. I was glad to see the first course arriving. It was spiced egg yolks. I had six; I was famished.

Once I'd satisfied my first hunger, I looked up to see who else was there. On my right was a pretty girl who introduced herself as the daughter of So-and-So the Judge; to my left, in order, were Tullia, Marrucinus, Marrucinus' wife (they were newly married, both being sixteen), and then a handsome but somewhat stupid-looking young man who was already talking about hunting wild pigs, his favorite sport.

I stayed quiet at first, after being introduced. I found I didn't know some of their expressions: I learned that I would have to say "Marky" when I meant the Roman Market; that Rome was never "Rome," it was just "the city"; and that even when addressing people I knew well I should use their last name. I wasn't "Aulus" any more, for instance, but "Spurinna."

Before long I found the courage to join in, deploying these expressions straight away and as often as possible. The wine was going round again, with a respectable amount of water mixed in. I nearly found myself drawn into an account of the last pig hunt I had been on – "got the beast myself with a throw of the javelin, right between the tusks." I was boring the Judge's daughter into a mild trance. And I was losing Tullia's attention, so I steered the conversation her way.

"You have to get up into the hills to find the big pigs," I said. "And that's a problem these days, at least in Etruria. Terrible trouble we've been having in our region."

Tullia's eyes swung round at the mention of Etruria. "I'm glad you brought that up," she said. "I have been dying to ask what is going on there. It could be important, you know. My father never forgets that Rome is more than just the city."

"Well, it's the threat to our tenants that brought me here," I said, and I told her the story of the feud between our farmers and the old soldiers, and of my uncle's murder. "It wouldn't be such a threat, I think, if they didn't have the leader they have. He's an old sergeant named Manlius. He stirs them up, always talking about redrawing the land."

"Manlius?" Tullia exclaimed. "Manlius, you said? *He's* the leader? You've had news of him?"

"News?" I replied. "Well, just six days ago he was shouting at me with his face as close to mine as yours is right now." I gave a quick account of our exchange, when Manlius had made his threats to take over the valley and enslave us. When I finished, Tullia paused and drew in her breath before replying.

"That was very dangerous, Spurinna. You don't know how dangerous. You say the old soldiers with him were armed? By Hercules!" At last she smiled. "Well, that's the old Roman courage of the countryside, the quality they're always praising in speeches. I didn't know it really existed."

"That's nothing," I said. "What you'll never believe is what my slave pointed out to me as we were traveling." I told her about the fortress-like army camp that Homer had spotted on the road, large enough for many, many more men than Manlius had with him at our house. She wasn't surprised at all, however, and didn't answer my questions about it. Soon she got up from her couch.

"Would you mind rising before the third course comes? It's peacock, but I would like to introduce you to my father."

She led me over to the host's table, and I had my first look at Cicero. He was a very ordinary looking man, with a round head and graying hair. He was in quiet conversation with a grave, ancient gentleman who wore robes of purple and gold – signs that in some remote period he had celebrated a Triumph over Rome's enemies. The others at the table gave the impression of austere self-control, though you could tell they were trying to overhear the Consul's words.

Tullia waited for her father to finish speaking, and then whispered something. He sat up, found me, and his eyes were immediately alert.

"Lucinus Spurinna. Of course, of course. I was grieved when your father died. And now your uncle has also departed? I am sorry to hear it. No, no letters from him, I would remember." His face clouded. But he came straight to the point. "My daughter tells me you have seen Manlius' camp, spoken with him, and come to us with word of his activities," he said. As I would later discover, Cicero tended to speak in units of three.

I bowed deeply. I confirmed my story, and answered his direct questions about the state of affairs in our valley and the feeling in Etruria. "We may know little of city politics, sir, but we know we are against Manlius, and we know we side with our Protector."

He smiled slightly at that. "And I with you, my young friend. But I must be frank. The Republic is in no mild danger, no insignificant peril, no trivial jeopardy. It is not Manlius who will lead Manlius' army. But I can say no more tonight. And if you would like to know more about politics in the city after all, come tomorrow to hear my speech to the Senate. Of course you can't come in, but my voice" – he betrayed a hint of self-satisfaction – "will be audible through the windows. Tullia will be glad to take you, I have no doubt."

I bowed deeply again. He thanked me for the information, and turned back to his guests.

I looked around for Tullia to lead me back to our table. To my surprise, she had edged over to speak with the strangest person at her father's table – a tall man of great bulk, not a Roman. He had a beard, a huge one that reached down to his waist, and red hair, and he was dressed very strangely. His toga (if that was the right word) was of a colorful pattern, and he wore a heavy silver star on his shoulder. Strangest of all, an elaborate tattoo of a stag decorated his cheek, in blue. There was no doubt about it, the man was a Celtic priest, a Druid, from the north of Italy. I had only heard of them, but they were said to be fantastic sorcerers. He spoke in a quiet sing-song, with a musical accent. He was friendly with Tullia, but when she turned back to me I noticed he was glancing nervously at Cicero. He seemed wary of the Consul.

"Who was that?" I asked Tullia.

"One of the ambassadors. Oh, I forgot. You don't know the news. Actually their story is much like yours, though on a larger scale," she smiled.

Back at our table, I asked her what her father had meant about the Republic being in no mild danger.

"Have you heard the name of Catiline?" she asked.

"Yes, there was a young man I met on the road who mentioned him. He's your father's enemy?"

"I suppose so," she answered. "He's the man behind Manlius, if that's enemy enough for you. He's had problems politically, and they might become everyone's problems soon. He makes speeches about canceling all debt, and some people love him for that. But it's really because he's deeply in debt himself. And he wants power. He wants it more than anything."

"Is he here?" I asked.

"Here, in this house? Of course not. But he's still in Rome. Half the people in this room are talking about him as we speak."

"But we're not?"

"I shouldn't say more than I've said, for now. My father thinks I get too interested. '*There rule, from palace cares remote and free*,' as the poet puts it."

"You sound just like my slave!" I laughed. But I added hastily, "I mean, my uncle's secretary, a Greek, named Homer. He's always quoting . . ."

"Homer?" she asked.

"No, the other poet, what's his name? Hesiod."

"You named your Greek slave 'Homer' when he likes Hesiod?"

"We didn't give him his name," I answered. "He comes from Athens where he worked in the philosophical university. He says he regrets that his old master there loved practical jokes."

At that moment, just as the final fruit was coming to our table, the steward appeared at Tullia's elbow and said that there was a strange Greek at the front who was asking for Lucinus Spurinna and behaving inexplicably.

"That's him!" I cried. "That must be Homer."

"I want to meet this literary slave of yours," Tullia said. "Let's find him."

We found Homer squatting on a large, tubular bag of sackcloth in the front hallway, with one of the ax-bearing guards standing over him. I embraced him and presented him to Tullia.

"It is a great honor," Homer said to her, bowing as far as he could but *not* rising from his seat on the bag.

"What's this?" I asked.

"This bag? Well, sir, it's part of my story," he said significantly, with the implication that it was a story he would like to tell.

"Come out of the hall, then," said Tullia, "and we'll hear it."

She led us off to a pantry near the kitchen, between the main hall and the dining room. Homer insisted on dragging his prize along himself – though it seemed very heavy – and planted himself right back on the bag when we had found a spot away from the guests. Not a quiet one, however. Waiters were bustling through continuously. Tullia and I each found a barrel to sit on. Homer looked exhausted. "It's from dragging this thing up the hill, sir, but it's nothing really."

"This man would like a cup of wine," said Tullia to a passing waiter.

"Thank you, madam. Yes, it's quite good," said Homer, when he took a sip. "Well, sir, madam," he began, "here it is."

He had spotted Volturcius in the square, abandoned me (that was not how he put it), and shadowed the man as far as his sedan-chair, which was waiting in an alley at the foot of the hill. "In an *alley*, sir, which you'll agree was itself rather suspicious." He had had a hard time keeping up with the sedan-chair bearers, what with the heat of the day, but they had not paid him the slightest attention.

"Not that we took the main streets, sir. It was all narrow lanes and so forth. And they led me straight to his house, though I had no idea where in the city we were 'til I found my way back."

At Volturcius' house, the sedan-chair had stopped, and Volturcius got out; but Homer was amazed to see a second man get out after him. "It was none other than Pantolemos, sir! Pantolemos, a man I knew from Athens! A philosopher, that is. They both went inside Volturcius' house. I found out at the sausage-seller's next door that they often went in together. But I couldn't very well knock on the door, so I waited in the shade across the street. Volturcius stayed inside, but the first person to come out – this was just after noon, sir – was old Pantolemos. He went down the back alley. Not much of a philosopher, of course. No doubt he was hired as a sort of house philosopher here, thirsting after riches like all those Epicureans."

I could have sworn the sackcloth bag Homer was sitting on seemed to move as he said this, but the dim light of the pantry played tricks on the eyes.

"You, I take it, do not belong to the Epicureans?" asked Tullia.

"Madam, I never have. I have always followed the other school," Homer replied. "But I had not seen Pantolemos since the old days in Athens. See what the years of dissolute living had done to him! Howbeit, sir, Pantolemos exited the house of Volturcius and . . . and he walked right over to the sausage-seller and ordered a hot sausage! I saw him eat it, sir!"

"An outrage, no doubt," I said.

"Well, it would be if you were an Epicurean, sir, and therefore a sworn vegetarian! How many arguments in Athens did we have about just that point? I'm surprised he didn't have it wrapped in the 'divine writings' of Epicurus himself, sir."

"Right, he had a sausage. Go on."

"Well, sir, realizing that this Pantolemos was now the house philosopher of the very man who – in all likelihood – is connected to the murder of your uncle, I thought, with the wise Hesiod, '*Seize not the goods, but take the god-sent chance.*'"

Again I was sure I saw the bag move, but it was likely just shifting under Homer's weight. He was sitting on it very heavily.

"How true," I said. "But come to the point, Homer."

"Yes, sir, the point. Well, as I was sitting in the shade and Pantolemos was munching his carnivorous snack, it occurred to me, sir, that the man must know every corner of Volturcius' house – even the slaves' quarters. And, therefore, if we are ever to get in there and find the truth about your uncle's murder, Pantolemos is essential. And he is a man who knows where his best interests lie. And, to be fair, sir, he is not a wholly mediocre philosopher."

"What are you driving at, Homer?"

"I only mean, sir, he is merely mistaken about the *cause* of philosophical virtue, not necessarily its effects."

"And . . . ?" This was tedious.

"And he's in this sackcloth bag here, sir."

5

What I Found with the Golden Dolls

I leapt to my feet. There was no doubt about it. Not only was the bag lumpy, but it was also *moving* and – yes – even groaning softly. I was astounded.

"Homer, you mean you've kidnapped that philosopher? And dragged him across Rome? And sat on him this last half hour?"

Homer looked unhappy. "I had to, sir."

"And why's that?" I cried. "He may be wrong about the . . . about what you said, Homer, but what you did is a crime! You're a kidnapper!"

"Actually, sir, since I happen to be a slave, it's my master who's responsible, legally."

"I was just getting to that!" I cried.

"But, sir, he knows Volturcius' house like the back of his hand."

"Shouldn't we let him out for some air?" suggested Tullia.

The philosopher Pantolemos was indeed looking bedraggled when we hauled him out of his bag. Homer had bound his ankles and wrists, too, and they looked sore when we took the rope off. With a nod he agreed not to shout out, so we also removed the gag. He shot Homer a hateful look, but was glad to accept a cup of wine from Tullia.

"The universities of Athens, in your day, must have been dangerous ground," she commented wryly.

"I came here for retirement, yes," he replied, scratching a long white beard.

"Well, I'm sorry for my slave's behavior," said I. "But I can't help that. You're involved in this now. So tell me, what do you know about Volturcius' trips to Faesulae?"

"Excuse me, sir," broke in Homer, "but I think it is usual to threaten the fellow with torture first and *then* ask questions."

Pantolemos glared at him, then turned to me while trying to control his fear. "Young man," he said, "surely you won't torture me! I may not be a Roman citizen, but by Zeus, I'm the guest of a Roman knight, a distinguished guest."

Homer made some sour remark about what he was distinguished for, but I cut him off.

"Now look here," I said to Pantolemos. "I'm a civilized person. We won't do anything unnecessary. But I want to find out what you know. And I must inform you," I threw in, "that you are in the house of the Consul of Rome right now."

"And your employer, Volturcius, may have links to an

enemy of the Roman People," added Tullia. I looked at her with surprise, but Homer seemed extremely pleased to hear it.

"But I really know nothing about Faesulae!" groaned Pantolemos. "That is, Volturcius owns some land there, everyone knows that, and he goes there, but I'm not his secretary, his agent, or anything. I just read the divine writings of Epicurus to him sometimes in the evening," he ended pitifully, "and I expound."

I asked more questions, but it really did seem Pantolemos was the last man you would trust with information about shady dealings or murder, and it was impossible to believe he had heard my uncle's name before.

"Homer, what now?" I asked.

"He can at least say how *we* can find the information, sir, if it exists." He turned to Pantolemos. "My dear old colleague, what is that back alley you were sneaking out from today? There was a terrible smell, if you remember."

The philosopher hated answering Homer, but he admitted that it was the garbage route. And, yes, he said, if you went in the back door there, no one could see you except the kitchen staff, and they would not be there tonight. A big key was hidden, he said, behind the ivy, and if you got past the door, you would see a corridor that led past the ball court. A flight of stairs at the end of the corridor led up to the study.

"And he uses the study?" broke in Tullia.

"Yes, yes, always a mess of papyrus sheets in there, great disorder," Pantolemos said. "And not a scroll of philosophy among them!" he added, warming up.

"Tullia," I said, "I'll bet my uncle's letters to your father are there. I can see them in my mind's eye, stacked up in a corner. We just need to get at them."

"If they haven't been burned," Homer observed.

"The letters, and other documents that are maybe even more important," Tullia replied. "Not to say that your tenants' troubles aren't important, I mean. And, Spurinna, I think you should go tonight."

"What? Tonight? Me?" I had been planning to lie low, scouting out Volturcius' house, and shadowing him around. I certainly had not been planning to break into his house by myself. "Maybe your father has agents he could send?"

"At this hour?" she answered. "No, it's already dark. And we don't have enough men these days, not with all the new developments. In all frankness," she ran her teeth over her lip, "I don't think my father would send agents on a hunch of mine. But Volturcius *is* a friend of Catiline's, or that's what I hear, and it fits with your interest in him. No. No, I will take care of this nice old man – he can stay here with the guards for several days – and you must go alone, or with this enterprising fellow," she said, indicating Homer.

Homer looked up brightly, but I shook my head. "I'll go alone," I said. "Homer, you look exhausted. But you can show me the way. I'm willing to try it." I looked back at Tullia. "And *you're* not coming, I suppose?"

She looked annoyed at this. "Well, I might, Spurinna, just to show you. But I can't leave the party now. And I have to help with the speech for tomorrow. Some other time, perhaps?"

"Sure thing," I said, somewhat angry to be sent off like this, as it seemed to me.

"I'll show you the way out," she replied with a grin, sending Pantolemos, happy enough now with another glass of wine, to a waiting room, and instructing the servants to burn the muddy bag from which he had emerged.

"So did you find us a place to stay?" I asked Homer when we had taken leave of Tullia and ventured out into the streets of Rome once more. It was a different scene than during the day. No one was out walking, and the night was almost chilly. I was excited enough not to care, however. Things seemed to be going almost too well. Not only had we located the man involved in the murder of my uncle, but I had talked to our Protector; and now I had a chance to show Tullia what I could do, infiltrating Volturcius' house. After such a string of success, what could really go wrong?

"A place to stay, yes, sir, I have," answered Homer. "By the square where I left you. I stopped there with the bag.

An extraordinary rent they asked for it, extraordinary. And a dirty place, sir, but we can clean it up."

He led us past the square. The building he showed me did look like it was falling apart. But from there we kept on towards Volturcius' house. It felt strange to be the only ones in the street: the buildings seemed even taller in the faint moonlight. We left the cobblestones far behind. They don't extend much past the Market and the temples in the city center. My feet were soon caked in cold muck.

"Just a little farther now, sir," Homer encouraged me, though he was far gone himself. He looked dead tired. "We turn right, I believe. Yes, and then past the public toilet. And left here. This is it now, Sicklemaker Street. And now, do you see the sausage shop sign up there, in red?"

Homer insisted that we should approach slowly and keep to the dark shadows. It was a good precaution. We weren't more than forty paces away when from behind us we heard the clank of hobnailed sandals, marching in step, a sudden clatter in the silent street. We melted into a gap in the wall of shops. The glow of torches passed us by, lighting the way for a large sedan-chair supported by the backs of sweaty porters.

I peered cautiously round the corner and watched the sedan-chair come to a stop. An aristocrat was entering Volturcius' house, together with two heavy men. I caught the clank of metal as they closed the door. The sedan-chair did not wait for them: once they were inside, it quickly disappeared down the street.

"Sir, are you sure it's wise to go in there tonight? That wasn't Volturcius in the sedan-chair," Homer said.

"I don't know if it's wise, Homer, but I'm going. Remember my uncle, and the blue poison on that letter. And Tullia would be glad to see some of those documents."

"Well, at least take this off, sir," said Homer, tugging at my bright white toga and unwinding it. "Your shirt is enough. Do you see where they went in? The alley is just before that, a little space between the buildings." He sighed. "Good luck, sir," he added, but I was already too intent on my next move to pay any attention to the Greek quotation he threw in. If I was not back in half an hour, we agreed, I would find him at the dingy apartment. He would look after my toga.

I'll say this: I am good at moving quietly when I choose. When you've often gone hunting in the hills, you have that advantage. I crossed Sicklemaker Street in total silence, and moved cautiously in the shadows on the other side, toward the opening next to Volturcius' house.

Homer had not been joking about the nasty smell of the alley. A narrow track snaked between heaps of rotting vegetables and bones, months and months of kitchen scraps. The reek was so strong, I reflected, that surely no Roman citizen would ever have set foot there – until I did, that is.

I heard a rustling sound ahead, as I rounded the corner. I realized – too late – that I was face to face with a dog. "Of course, the night guard dog," I thought bitterly, and I half turned to run. But the dog only gave a low growl. He didn't bark, and now he seemed less large. He was big-boned, yes, but he was starving, and too keen on the magnificent feast of bones he was holding in his jaws to bother with me. I crept on past him.

There in the wall of the house, just as Pantolemos had told us, was a small door, lower than my shoulders, with a keyhole. Beyond the door, the wall seemed to turn into an outer wall of a private garden, for ivy was growing over it and part way up the house itself. I reached behind the ivy, and found a little hollow where a brick had broken off. Nestled inside was the iron key, just as Pantolemos had promised.

Gently, I slid it into the lock, and tried to turn it quietly. It wouldn't turn! Five times I brought it out and tried again. Nothing moved. Could it be the wrong key? Could the lock have rusted since Pantolemos used it this afternoon? I finally gave it a violent twist; and with what seemed an ear-splitting scrape (though it could not have been so loud) the iron key turned and the door opened.

It was as dark as the underworld inside. Five steep steps led down to a passageway, which smelt strongly of cooking herbs. I closed the door behind me and descended. My eyes adjusted quickly. There was lamplight filtering through windows high on the right-hand wall of the corridor. It seemed the corridor ran rather lower than the ground level of the house, and that lamp-lit room was the ball court.

"Point, a point for Volturcius!" came a cry from the room. It shook me terribly, for it was the first sign that indeed there was someone in the building. Craning my neck, I could see the sandaled feet in the ball court: two pairs of feet, though I heard three voices, together with the smack of the polished wooden ball upon the catchers' palms. "Game point," remarked a shy, dry voice. "This is it now."

Creeping, I passed two rooms on my left that looked like small kitchens. Beyond that, there was a black emptiness. I could just make out steps. It was the spiral staircase, again just where Pantolemos had told us. Though I could see nothing as I climbed up, I could sense the cold stone, and as careful as I was my footfalls brought uncanny echoes.

After two tight spirals, I reached another corridor on the next story. All was quiet, except for the smack of the wooden ball in the court, which I could now hear more distinctly. According to Pantolemos, the study should be close by; and there it was, just opposite the top of the stairs, on the far side of the passage. I crept to the door. Lamplight was filtering through the cracks in the wooden floorboards, and I could clearly see that the room was covered in papyrus sheets.

I entered the study. Surely my uncle's intercepted letters lay nearby.

The problem was finding them in the mess. If Volturcius had thrown all the scrolls and sheets up in the air and let them fall where they liked, there could not have been more confusion. There were no stacks, no piles. Here and there lay chewed-up reed pens. On a shelf I saw a jumble of strange figurines – enchanted dolls for evil magic, from Egypt, painted with dull gold.

Laughter burst from below. The study was directly above the ball court, it seemed. A man clapped, then many people seemed to be entering the court. Chairs scraped on the stone floor, and cries of greeting and the hum of chitchat filled the silence. Not only was the house inhabited, but now it appeared to be hosting a large number of guests. I did not stop to wonder why they should be gathering in the ball court.

Instead I concentrated on my task, frantically searching through as many papers as I could. There was an endless series of them. Letters from creditors, threatening to haul Volturcius to court and ruin his political career; anxious letters from friends, wondering how the investment they were making together was coming along; letters from Volturcius, begging shamelessly for more time to repay, or in fact for further loans of an immense amount – five times what our whole property was worth. The man had ambitious plans.

Then there were the astrological tables, diagrams in colored ink whose intricate arcs and bisecting angles promised to reveal the fate of whoever could understand them. There were maps of animal organs, too, precisely labeled with odd abbreviations, for soothsaying, and prayers to recite in languages I did not recognize, and a set of knuckle-bones inside a stack of revenue charts. I went through everything. Whenever the papyrus sheets and scrolls rustled and crackled, my hands clenched and I held my breath. But the conversations in the room beneath me never stopped.

Nowhere, however, could I see my uncle's or Homer's handwriting. I scanned sheet after sheet, scroll after scroll for mention of "Spurinna," "Manlius," "Etruria," or "Faesulae" – finding this last in one crumpled scroll, but only with respect to how much more rent the leatherworkers there could be forced to pay for Volturcius' protection. There was nothing – not until I lifted a dusty jumble of miniature scrolls and caught the glint of blue glass.

My hand trembled as I picked it up. The golden magic dolls seemed to leer at me through the darkness. The small flask, stopped with a piece of wood, was not dusty, and with the sixth sense that tells us when an object has recently been touched by human hands, I knew that the flask did not belong with the neglected documents and magic charts. It had been purposely hidden beneath them. It was a flask of thick blue liquid, bright and shiny even in the gloom, and I knew it was the poison that had stained the letter Homer found, the poison that had brought death to my poor uncle.

Conspiracy for Murder

I will not say that it was sadness for my uncle that made me silently choke back tears, and it wasn't rage either. The feeling that surged through me was unmistakable. Suddenly my hesitation and my doubt were gone. I saw everything with terrible clarity – my duty was to get revenge.

At that moment, however, the chitchat of the guests in the ball court ceased. The silence was sudden and profound. I froze, still clutching the blue flask in my outstretched hand, not daring to move. Then someone began to speak formally, pronouncing each word distinctly, just the way my Aunt Hercna used to speak to the tenants once a month. After the voice said, "And we thank our friend Volturcius for again opening his fine house to our gathering," there was a murmur of agreement and then the speech – that is the word for it, an authentic political speech – began:

"Gentlemen," the voice continued, "friends, Senators, and Roman knights, this will not be our last meeting. But it will be the last before our great enterprise is brought to fulfillment. So I will speak plainly tonight to all of you together. If I did not trust the honor of each and every one of you, I would not be here, and I would not be speaking here tonight; but neither would I have undertaken this adventure in the first place. I would not have been so bold."

I stood like a statue, for there was an easy confidence and good will in the voice that commanded you to listen. But somehow I felt the man was being less than straightforward already, despite what he assured his listeners.

"We want the same thing, gentlemen, and this common goal of ours is the proof of our friendship. We are Romans, certainly, and we are pleased when the nations, the princes, the kings of the earth pay this city their taxes and their tribute. So they should, and so they must. We want the glory of Rome forever. But *we* should rule it. We *must* rule it!

"By now, one thing is clear. Though Rome flourishes, *we* cannot flourish as things stand. The Senate rules, and Cicero rules. They claim they rule for the good of Rome. But, gentlemen, *we* are the good of Rome! To them, we are merely the instruments of their power. They will be *our* instruments! To them, we are mere fools. They will be *our* fools! To them, we are slaves. They will be *our* slaves! And which one of us here tonight would not prefer to own this city? Who would not prefer exile to insult? Who would not prefer death to disrespect?"

There was a mounting murmur of approval – from many more voices than I had thought were present, at least two dozen. And for a moment I myself wavered. The power of that voice was almost irresistible. He seemed like an honest man, a man only asking for what he deserved. Then a young voice cried. "That's it, Catiline! You speak for us! Good for Catiline!"

My heart leapt into my throat when I heard that name. Could this really be the voice of the most dangerous man in Rome? The pickpocket at the inn had praised him, Tullia had called him the man behind Manlius, an enemy of the Roman People. But suddenly he was more than a name. He was standing in the room below me, with only the floorboards between us. I almost wished that Homer were by my side. What could I do except listen?

"While they prosper, gentlemen," the voice of Catiline continued, "while they prosper, we are laughed at in the street. While they conquer the world, we cannot even conquer the slaves who should worship us. In short, we have nothing to lose, and everything to gain. And now the hour has come to seize the prize, the prize that belongs to those who are not afraid to conquer.

"If you wish, I will be a simple soldier. If you wish, I will be your leader. If you wish, I will be the Consul Rome has dreamed of. But if you do not remember much of what I say tonight, remember this much: We are facing ruin already, we are confronted this very night by a hundred dangers, but we are working now for victory, for glory, for immeasurable riches, and for a fame that will not die. A new Rome, a Rome without the Senate, without aristocratic shame, without Cicero, is waiting to be born. And we ourselves have waited long enough!"

He was finished, and though the men listening could not cheer in the quiet house, their grunts of approval went on for what seemed an eternity to me. There was an ugly fierceness in their agreement. I lowered my arms to my sides, terrified that they might hear my shirt brush against my skin.

"You speak well, Catiline!" said the same young voice. "But that should not be the end of it. We have one army in Etruria, but we need another here. If we would only proclaim to the whole city that we will free the slaves, then . . ."

"Free the slaves?" cried Catiline. "Free the scum of the earth? What do you take me for? I am not here to liberate, my young friend! I am here to conquer! And we have that other army already, though you may not know it. Yes, we do. And here I call upon my true friend, our common friend, a friend of Rome."

A silence fell again, and I heard someone walk to the middle of the room beneath me. He began to speak in a low tone and with a foreign accent, so quietly that I could not make out much. But my pulse began to throb in my ears, for there was no mistaking the sing-song lilt of his Latin. It was the Druid I had seen lying at Cicero's own table earlier that evening, talking with Tullia, looking nervously at the Consul who was his host.

"... do what we can," I heard the Druid saying, "... with both armies, if you think of the total ... the advantages on both sides, and I have ... the other ambassadors ... certain assurances will, of course, be ... because of the needful supplies ... ten thousand warriors ... confident of our sincerest thanks," he ended, to what seemed to be sighs of relief from the other men. Were they themselves afraid of the Druid?

"And you have consulted the gods, the local gods?" broke in the dry voice I had heard before, playing ball in the court. "Surely you have not neglected the proper rituals, the test of the animals?"

"Volturcius," said Catiline, "your concerns are natural, and our friend has naturally consulted the gods. They have confirmed our inevitable victory. But now give us your report from Faesulae. Will Manlius march, if the Druid's Celtic warriors are ready?"

"Manlius will not fail us. He has collected two legions. They will march when the moon is full," answered Volturcius.

"And in secrecy? You remember that at our last meeting we discovered that Cicero" – Catiline nearly spat the name – "was receiving information about Manlius from Etruria, from that wretched landowner and his farmer spies. That has stopped?"

"The landowner has stopped," answered Volturcius hoarsely. "The sad news came only two days ago when I was there. The poor man passed away, thanks to our little blue ally."

There were some chuckles at this. My hands began to shake uncontrollably with fury. Volturcius was joking about the murder of my uncle! I had not really doubted his treachery before, what with the blue flask, yet . . . and with that the flask slipped from my fingers, bounced off a papyrus roll, and fell tinkling to the floor.

"What was that?" came the voice of Catiline below. "What was that noise? It came from the kitchens."

"No, from upstairs!" cried several other voices. I could feel twenty necks craning to stare through the ceiling under feet.

"I sent the kitchen slaves to bed, I assure you," broke in Volturcius. "It's the mice, gentlemen. My study is above us and the mice come to chew the papers. Please, please be seated."

"Very well," said Catiline with some hesitation. "Let us continue. This landowner may be no further trouble, thanks to you, Volturcius," he went on, "but hear this, my friends. I am not satisfied. It is time that Cicero himself was dealt with. Only yesterday he blocked our move at Praeneste. All of the gladiators we sent there have been taken by his forces. I found out today. Our best fighters are prisoners. He is energetic, and he knows more about us than we suspect, I am sure of it. But we still have some gladiators, do we not?"

"About twenty," someone answered.

"Good," said Catiline. "We will not need that many. But I want volunteers. The dawn is not far off now. Two of you will go to pay your respects to Cicero this morning. You will take gladiators, five of the best we have left, and you will pretend to consult him on affairs of state. Mention my name if you have to. Say that you will give him information. And then, in his own hall, you can cut him down."

There was silence at this. I gasped, and the young voice below exclaimed, "But you can't kill the Consul! By Hercules, the Senate will never stand for it – that risks everything!"

"The Consul?" cried Catiline, his clear tone suddenly hoarse. "You idiot," he rasped, "it is *I* who am the Consul! I would have been Consul these last ten months if it weren't for Cicero's tricks, and I would be Consul next year if they hadn't all stood against me during the election. Cicero is no Consul, I tell you that. And do not worry about the Senate. In three days the city will be burning. We will put the torch to it, as planned – Greek quarter, the Slaves' quarter, and Pomegranate Street – and you worry about the Senate! The Senate will be ours for the taking, once Rome is burning."

My mind was reeling. First the poison, then Catiline's own voice and his terrible speech, then the treacherous Druid, and Volturcius laughing about my uncle. Now it was to be murder for Cicero: I had to act. I scooped up a pen from Volturcius' papers and began scratching frantically across the back of one of his astrological charts. The Greek quarter . . . the Slaves' quarter . . . Pomegranate Street . . . Praeneste . . . all the names I could remember. I underlined *Volturcius*. Whatever plan I had for my personal revenge would have to wait. Tullia had to know what I now knew. The men below went on with their conspiracy, but I was running out of time.

"I shall go to Cicero," someone said, volunteering for murder. "And my friend here shall come with me. A Senator and a Roman knight – both Orders shall have a hand in it, with the gladiators."

"Very good," said Catiline. "But you must be thorough. The whole house, you understand? And if they . . ."

"That's not mice now," someone interrupted. "That scratching, do you hear that? I know mice, by Hercules, and that's not . . ."

"That's the floorboards!" exclaimed Catiline. "I knew it, there's someone up there! Mice indeed, Volturcius! Who's your spy upstairs, I'd like to know?"

"There's no spy!" protested Volturcius. "No one can get in my door. We're safe, and I would never . . ."

"Go and find out," Catiline ordered, and instantly men were up and moving.

But I had left the study far behind.

I had bolted for the corridor by the time they heard the floorboards, the astrological chart in my hand, but I had no time to pick up the blue flask. I did not dare descend the spiral staircase now: I could already hear footsteps coming up, and I caught the hint of torchlight on the stairs. To my right were bedroom doorways. There was a narrow window at the end of the corridor to the left, but it was barred with wooden shutters.

I raced for the window and tore off the wooden latch. The window was set high in the wall, but I hoisted myself up to the sill. The window was narrow, too – a full-grown man's shoulders could never have fit. I barely got through it myself.

And, by Hercules, it was a long way down. I could hardly see the garbage alley and the kitchen scraps in the darkness beneath. I could hear feet racing to the top of the stairs and into the study. Yet just as I was about to jump – probably to my death – I saw that the garden's ivy had grown up as far as the window. I seized the trunk of the vine with both hands.

It tore away from the wall! No sooner did the roots tear than I grabbed a new hold beneath them, lowering myself handful by handful until I tumbled backward into space. The garbage broke my fall, but it was all I could do not to scream as I landed. Bits of bone and wood jabbed into my side, but I was on my feet at once. I thanked the gods the hungry dog had disappeared. And then I ran.

Not the way I had come, past the front of Volturcius' house, but the other way. Would the alley lead me somewhere? Or would I have to bury myself in the trash and hope they did not find me?

I reached the next street. A wooden fence barred the way, but the blood was pumping in my veins and for the moment I felt no pain in my side. I sprang to the top. Just then I heard a voice behind me. A man was speaking from the narrow window I had left behind.

"Nothing here. Double-check the other way," he said. "Just the wind, and these old shutters."

He latched the shutters as I swung over the fence to the street beyond. I had escaped, and I had my scribbled notes. I was safe. Unfortunately, I was also lost.

Nothing could force me to double back down the alley to the front of the house. I would have to find my way around, and it seemed likely that the street I was now on would run parallel to Sicklemaker Street. Yet though this new street began in the same direction, it gradually veered to the right. I scanned the shops on the left, but there was neither a cross street nor another alley. I was being headed off, down the hill towards the clothmakers' district.

It was a labyrinth. A turn to the left led only to another faceless, impassable block of buildings. I hoped for an empty square where I could get a feeling for the direction of Cicero's house, but when I finally found one I could see nothing beyond the lofty third stories of the blocks. There was no one to give directions, except for sleeping drunks and a group of men who could not have looked more sinister if every one of them had been a Catiline. I pressed on blindly, alone.

I could feel the change in the air, the breath of dawn, by the time I finally reached the cobblestones again. From here I could guess the way to the Market. But I was panting with exhaustion and bathed in chilly sweat as I shuffled over that vast empty space, ghostly at the hour poised between the old night and the new day. The tops of the gigantic marble columns of the temples floated high above me. "The Marky," I heard Tullia say in my head. "You must say 'Marky,' Spurinna." And I thought of how I had dreamed of seeing the Market during the manhood festival in the Spring. How far away the world of school and farm and harvesting now seemed, where everything except our house was built of wood, and no one had ever seen a cobblestone.

Now that I had found the Market, I knew which way to go. It was not far to the hill where Cicero lived, the Palatine hill. But I had lost precious time. I sprinted with a final effort up the steep street.

When I reached the doors of his house, I gasped. Where were the guards who had been there in the afternoon? I pounded on the doors for what seemed like forever. At last someone called out from inside.

"What in the name of Numa is this blasted racket?" I was being watched through the observation hole. "Who in the name of – Spurinna? It can't be! Again!"

It was the scornful steward.

"Yes, it's me," I cried. "Open up, in the name of Jupiter! You must wake Cicero . . . you must wake the Consul! Let me in, I have urgent . . ."

With a dull *plunk*, the heavy wooden bolt struck the marble floor of the hall, and the iron doors creaked open.

"What's this now?" whispered the steward. "Young man, do you have any idea what time . . ."

"I do, yes. And if you don't wake up Tullia before I get my hands on you, I'll . . ."

I stopped. No time for another squabble. The steward was biting his lip with annoyance and contempt. It suddenly struck me that I must look ridiculous, even more ridiculous than when I had shown up with the horse and the donkey. Now I was sweaty, covered in bits of garbage, and notably – as far as the steward was concerned – *not* covered in the toga of a citizen paying his morning respects.

"Get Tullia." I repeated. "Your master's life may depend on it!"

He obeyed reluctantly, leaving me alone there, with the dark sky now growing pale. I heaved the wooden bolt back across the iron doors, and collapsed beside them.

But Tullia was not long in coming.

"Spurinna, what in heaven's name . . . ? Are you all right?" she called, hurrying across the hall to my side. She pulled me to my feet.

She was wearing a white sleeping gown. I saw her hair was undone and her eyes were sleepy; but I must have looked worse myself because she said, "You look absolutely terrible! Are you hurt? Did you get inside that traitor's house?"

"Where is Homer?" I asked.

"He came back, but he said he waited near Volturcius' house and you didn't come out, so he left to see if you had gone to the room he rented. He looked tired. But, Spurinna, are you going to tell me what happened or not?"

I gave her an incoherent account. Her brows knit with concern, as I babbled incoherently. "They are coming to kill your father this morning . . . two men volunteered . . . going to pretend it's political advice . . . gladiators with them . . . I have some names, information scribbled on this chart. . . ." She grew instantly alert, told me to wait, rushed off, and brought back two guards with their long-handled axes.

"We must be ready for them," she said in a low voice. "Can you stand? Will you lie down?"

"I'm staying," I said.

"Stay by the door," she said. "I'm going for the rest of the guard. Steward," she barked, "wake up the Consul. Spurinna, if they come, you must delay them. Do you hear me? Delay them til I come with more guards. You can talk? Then you must delay them. No one comes in, alright? No one!"

And she was gone in a flash of the white gown.

The silence afterward was unbearable. A rooster crowed the dawn, followed by another, and another. A chorus of roosters. Where were the other guards?

I turned to the two guards with me. They looked as frightened as I felt.

"Who is coming, sir?" one asked.

"Assassins," I told them bluntly. "We must protect the Consul."

It was the right thing to say. The first guard brightened and gripped his ax: protecting the Consul was the purpose of his life. But the second guard looked less steady.

"Assassins, like at Praeneste yesterday?" he asked. "Those were gladiators, you know, the best of the Arena. That's what they say . . . champions, sir. It took two hundred men to stop sixty."

"We're not two hundred men, but we can stop them," I replied, wondering how foolish that sounded. "Just be as tough with them as you were with me when I first showed up. We'll be all right then, don't you think?"

At this the second guard nodded nervously. "Deliveries do go round the back," he said, smiling bleakly.

"That's right," I said. "And don't forget this is the *Consul's* house."

At that moment there were footsteps in the street. It seemed to be only one pair of sandals, but what if there were many walking softly? One loud pair of sandals, and others treading silently? Someone called out a cheerful "Good morning!" and then, to my horror, there came a polite knock at the door, and the sound of something being placed on the ground. When neither I nor the guards made any answer – they were following my lead – the knock was repeated, more forcefully. For a second I paused, and the thought crossed my mind that these were perhaps the final minutes of my life.

Then I sang out, "Who is it?"

"It's me, Laurentius."

I didn't recognize the voice from Volturcius' house. And the name 'Laurentius' was not in the notes I had scribbled in the study. But there had been many conspirators, and not all of them had spoken up.

"The Senator? And what brings you here so early this morning?"

A nervous laugh. "Senator? No, it's me, the baker, Laurentius. It's me, the baker."

The baker? The morning bread? He would get a shock if we opened the doors now: two guards ready to kill and one bedraggled young man. But could I trust his claim? Or would Catiline's assassins be trying to pass for bakers?

I stepped to the doors and peered out the observation hole. I could see, though not too well, but not be seen. In the street, to my surprise, stood a kindly looking, small, middle-aged man. He was holding a basket of pastries under his arm, and he was smiling uneasily, glancing from side to side. It was indeed a baker.

Then a hairy hand reached around to clamp the little man's mouth shut. Another hand, grasping a knife, thrust a blade deep into the baker's throat. Blood poured down his shirt, splashing the pastries, and he fell, gurgling. Behind him I caught the golden glint of a gladiator's polished helmet.

Closer to the door, but out of my line of sight, someone coughed slightly and said, in a tired, almost languid tone, "Hello. Would you let us in? We have come to wish the Consul a good morning."

Siege and Speech

Now, I am not trying to boast about what happened. I would be the first one to admit, if you asked me in private, that I didn't do much that morning. But when I saw the baker's body fall and I heard them saying "Hello" on the other side of that front door, the blood rushed up to my brain and it hit me: "*Aulus, now you find out if you're a Roman like your father. Are you going to faint, or are you going to stand there and keep on talking?*"

There were only the two guards with me. They had their axes, and also the heavy javelins that soldiers use. Of course, they didn't know what had happened outside the door. I stepped back from the door to join them and whispered, "Get your weapons ready." But I was indeed afraid. I had come to Rome hoping I might, after all, see gladiators in the Arena. I never dreamed I would be fighting them myself.

Behind us in the house I could hear Tullia calling out to her men to watch the side door. She was stationing men at the back of the house. But where were the others she had promised – the reinforcements? How long could the wooden bolt hope to keep these 'visitors' out?

It was up to me to speak. I spoke. "Let me wish you a good morning, gentlemen. May I ask who we have the pleasure of welcoming this morning?"

Two men gave their names: a Senator and a Roman knight, the same ones who had volunteered at Volturcius' house. There was a note of impatience in their voices.

"And you're here to speak with Marcus Tullius Cicero, I understand?" That was the best I could think of. Surely they would grasp that I was stalling?

"That's right, just like we said. Don't be rude now. Let us in, and fetch your master."

"May I ask how many have come with you? We would like to offer you some small refreshment." I was running out of ideas. It was the height of rudeness to keep a Senator waiting in the street.

"Just ourselves and our secretaries, naturally. Political business. Now, when will you open this door, slave?"

At that moment Tullia rushed up. She had four more guards with her. I drew my finger across my throat to show that I was speaking to the would-be murderers. But she was never one to back off.

"This is Tullia, the Consul's daughter," she called out. "I am sorry to keep you waiting, gentlemen. We are somewhat slow this morning. Surely you wouldn't like to embarrass a young woman who is fixing her hair?"

I grabbed a javelin from one of the guards. Our little farce could not last long.

"We can wait inside, madam. It's cold out here."

"I assure you," she answered, "it is just as cold in here."

"Then we won't wait at all!" the Roman knight shouted, losing his temper. He barked an order and straightaway the iron doors groaned as the weight of five gladiators slammed against them.

"This is outrageous!" shouted Tullia. "This is the Consul's house!" She was red with anger, her fists clenched. I pulled her back as the doors heaved again. The wooden bolt was about to give way. The guards growled and clenched their teeth, raising their axes. And then, with the third slam of the gladiators' bodies against the hapless bolt, the wood split with a resounding crack and the doors flew open.

Suddenly they were inside – seven of them – the two 'visitors' with daggers, and five fighting champions in ferocious-looking armor. One was flourishing a net and a three-pronged pike, just as he would in the Arena; two of them wielded huge, heavy maces and wore masks with slits for eyes. The others, in shining golden helmets and breast-plates, just had swords. In a pool of blood behind them lay their first victim, the poor baker, Laurentius.

There was no more talk, but the standoff lasted a little longer as both sides sized each other up, staring like statues. "Back, traitors!" I cried, flourishing my javelin. The six guards and I had formed a ring about the door, but we were spread thin.

The net-man was the first to make a move. With a flick of the wrist he sent the heavy net flying, right in the face of the biggest guard. The man swung his ax to knock it aside, but too late: he was entangled, and the net-man's pike flashed in, jabbing the guard's shoulder. To his left our next guard swung his ax against the net-man, but the Arena-fighter parried the blow with the shaft of his pike, wrenching the second guard off balance. They tumbled together, struggling

"Now get them!" cried the Senator – an older man, neatly dressed but unshaven, whose voice I recognized from Volturcius' house – and the next gladiator, one with a golden helmet, sprang to the gap in the circle where the first guard had fallen. Slashing his sword, he rounded on the guard to his right and sliced the man's arm. The guard's ax clattered to the marble floor.

I didn't hesitate. With all my strength I sent my heavy javelin whistling through the air, right on target. The point found the gap between the golden helmet and the breast-plate. The gladiator shrieked and collapsed as the javelin pierced his neck. I reached quickly for another weapon.

But the charge had stopped dead. The others stared with shock at their fallen comrade. Just then the net-man freed himself from the guard he was wrestling and bolted for the door. His comrades stood stock still. The momentum was all ours.

"Drive them back!" I shouted, and our three remaining guards raised their axes.

It was all but over, however. Mute, their feet shuffling cautiously across the marble floor, the others backed out the door. I caught the look of venomous hatred on the Senator's face, but then he too was gone. The mace-wielding gladiators had not even swung their hideous weapons.

The iron doors clanged shut again as the guards threw themselves against them. The guard with the bleeding arm kicked at the fallen gladiator, but it was pointless – the man was dead.

"Spurinna! Aulus!" cried Tullia, throwing her arms around my neck. "You did it! I can't believe it! You did it!" There were tears in her eyes, perhaps of amazement, for like me she must have felt it was all over for us.

"What's this? Daughter, who is this young man?" called a sleepy voice. It was Cicero, coming down the stairs. He wore a chain-mail shirt. "What do I hear about . . ." he began, but stopped when he saw the dead assassin, still anonymous in his gleaming golden helmet.

"Father, oh Father! You should have seen it! Spurinna, he stopped them, right here in our hall! It was Catiline, Father, Catiline's men. They came to kill you."

"Spurinna, it's you!" he exclaimed. "I'm sorry, I didn't recognize you. What's this Tullia says? A dead man in my hall?" His mouth was open. But he controlled himself quickly. "Well now, there is not much time before my speech. Come to breakfast. You must tell me what has happened, what has eventuated, indeed exactly what has come to pass."

It was a long story. I had not slept, and Tullia kept interrupting, either to clarify points of fact or to congratulate me again. But I protested that it was nothing: her father was my Protector, after all. Cicero was grateful for the business with the assassins, certainly, but he was mostly interested in the other things I'd heard at Volturcius' house. Breakfast was not long enough, and in the end he asked me to accompany him to his speech in his sedan-chair – he had even had new clothes cut for me while we ate.

"Well," Cicero concluded, leaning on a cushion as we were carried along, "you've only been in the city since yesterday, and I dare say it's been exciting for you. And profitable for me. It is agreeable to be your Protector, Spurinna. The information about these plans to burn the city – burn Rome! – is remarkable, exceptional, extraordinary. And to think this man is still taking part in the councils of the Republic!"

"Catiline, sir?"

"Yes, Catiline. Indeed, Catiline. He will be among the Senators today, if I guess correctly. But not for long." He looked out the side of the sedan-chair as it passed into the crowd, his bodyguards clearing a way through the streets so that we went much more swiftly than I had thought possible. Every eye was bent on us, it seemed, and Cicero waved with dignity, like a good politician, and the people called his name with approval, or offered him their free advice. Some caught sight of the chain mail he was wearing, and then they cursed these times of death and danger.

"Not for long," Cicero repeated, fiddling with the scroll of his speech. Then, decisively, he put the scroll aside. "Not much use for this now, is there, daughter? Time for that old Roman virtue, spontaneous eloquence." He smiled at me. "Catiline's ears will truly burn today," he said, chuckling.

Part of me wanted to ask Cicero what good a speech could do when they had just tried to murder him, but Tullia caught my eye. She seemed to take a grim pleasure at her father's plan. She also refused to let go of my wrist for the whole ride.

We reached the spot where the Senate was to meet, the Temple of Jupiter the Savior, and climbed out. It was uphill for the last hundred paces, but Cicero wished to walk it. Once we had emerged, I saw why. Not only was the sun shining in a perfect autumn sky of deep blue, but a dense crowd of people formed a human alley to the Temple, an avenue of togas. When Cicero appeared they went wild, chanting his name. Tullia and I slipped to the side.

"Let's take advantage of this," she whispered, grabbing my hand. She led me up the slope and over to the Temple of Minerva, where a side wall faced the larger Temple of Jupiter. We climbed onto the narrow top of the wall. "Here we are," she said. "And there's hardly anyone here! This is the best spot for listening. Isn't it more quiet? But don't fall off, Aulus."

We sat there with our feet dangling over the side, the crowd beneath us. There was more cheering now as another figure made his way up, striding briskly. He was about Cicero's age, but balding, and he was very tall.

"That's Julius Caesar," said Tullia. "Handsome, isn't he? But not a friend of ours, for now. He's a mystery. Very popular, though" she added grudgingly.

Other Senators in purple-striped togas arrived, one after the other, meeting with various levels of approval from the crowd. Last of all, a lonely figure approached, and the cheers subsided completely, except from one section where some younger men were gathered. He paused at the front steps of the temple, turning to survey the city and the mass of citizens, and I noted the pride in the way he carried himself, and the abrupt swing of his head.

"That's him," said Tullia, lowering her voice involuntarily. "The one who sent the men this morning."

Catiline.

He took the steps two at a time and vanished into the sacred precinct.

"Does he look like you thought he would?" she asked.

"Yes, he does," I nodded.

I looked over to take in the view Catiline had just surveyed. A strange way to be seeing the city – from the heights – for the first time. How had I become mixed up in all this? I could see three of Rome's seven hills from our perch, rising like waves in the ocean of brown buildings, with the Roman Market there between, far below, its cobblestones gleaming in the sun and its temples like children's dollhouses for the gods. To the north the river turned back and forth, lazily rippling past the world of wood and marble. For all the Romans claimed the Tiber as their friend, I doubted if the river would make much of the crisis of our days. Had it not seen every kind of politics already? In the distance the sky met the green land in a remote haze of white, and I imagined the gods themselves watching, waiting, and wondering what Cicero would say in Jupiter's own temple that day. They at least were willing to pay attention, by all accounts.

"Do you like the view?" said Tullia. "I'll show you the Market later."

"Let the Consul speak," a mighty voice proclaimed from where the Senate sat, and straightaway the murmurs of the gathered people ceased, for they could hear every word.

There was a pause.

"How long now . . ." came Cicero's voice, quite different from the voice of the Cicero in the sedan-chair. Now it was the voice of the Consul, stern and uncompromising. "How long will you test our patience, Catiline?

How far will your uncontrollable rashness go? Does it mean nothing to you that guards roam the streets, that this Senate frowns as one man upon you, that the people flock to hear its verdict?"

The crowd gave one great roar at this, and immediately grew quiet once again.

"And yet, Catiline, you still live. You live, and every day brings greater proof of your treachery. Gentlemen of the Senate, I wish to be kind. I wish to be just. But at this moment I am willing, in front of everyone, to charge myself with laziness. After all, have we not had word that there are military camps – military camps! – in Etruria, built for an army that will march on Rome? Did I not predict in this Senate that Manlius would take up arms against us? Did I not state that you, Catiline, would seek to burn this eternal city to the ground? Yet though you may deserve death, Catiline, I will continue to be lazy, and you will continue to live, so long as there is a single man who dares to claim that you are innocent."

"Cicero, Cicero, Cicero!" chanted the crowd, and then returned to listening intently.

"Come now, Catiline, and let us glance at your activities last night. Then you will see how much more vigilant I am for the safety of the Republic than you are for its destruction."

Tullia nudged me and whispered, "This is you coming up."

"I declare now, in this Senate, that you were in Sicklemaker Street last night, Catiline. To be precise, in the house of Volturcius, with a band of your fellow traitors. Do you dare to deny it? Then why are you silent? I will prove it, if you deny it! There and then you plotted the arrival of Manlius. There and then you chose the neighborhoods that you would burn. There and then you asked for volunteers to come pay me a visit with their swords this very morning. Yet I had word of this; we threw them back, we closed the door; your friends fled to find you."

"For shame, for shame!" chanted the crowd, shaking their fists. "Murderers, murderers of the Consul!"

"Your plots are laid bare, Catiline," the Consul continued. "Your hopes are empty. You have tried to ruin Rome. Now it is your reputation that lies in ruins. What do you have left? Shall I ask the Senate? No, for they are passing their verdict as we speak. Their silence is their verdict. Go forth freely, then, from the city you would like to burn. Manlius is waiting for you. Go forth, and liberate this city from the fear of you that is already burning it. Go forth and take your traitors, your accomplices, your conspirators with you. Make war upon your homeland from outside these sacred city walls, not inside them."

"No, no, don't let him go! Take him now, destroy him!" shouted the crowd.

"Here is proof of my forbearance, Catiline. Here we are, the Consul asking the enemy of Rome simply – to go. For if I had you killed, Catiline, there would be some who would say that I was just removing you as a rival. But here is why you live. You will not confess among us here. But when you go to Manlius, and lead that traitorous army against the city we love – to burn, pillage, and ravage it – then we will have your confession. Go forth, Catiline, to your ruinous war. Take the field against us if you dare. Save this Republic, and destroy your fellow traitors."

"Send him out, show him the door!" came the calls from the crowd. "Exile, exile for Catiline!"

"And you, Jupiter," Cicero went on, turning (I imagined) to the mighty statue of the king of the gods inside the temple, "you whom we rightly call the savior of this city, you who specialize in murderers and slaughterers, it is you who will administer your justice to this man, to this Catiline, and punishment to his conspirators – both while they are still alive, and then for all eternity when they are dead."

It was a brilliant finish. The crowd went absolutely crazy. The tension had been building through the speech, and now they threw their purses in the air, chanting the Consul's name, shouting for joy. People were joining hands, and some were dancing. The celebration grew and grew, the roar went on and on.

Inside the temple there was applause and a more dignified cheer for Cicero. And then Catiline tried to speak – I could hear his voice, familiar from the night before, starting sentence after sentence in vain – but the

Senate's murmuring intensified, drowning him out. They were denouncing him, refusing to allow him to speak, urging him to leave the city, just as Cicero had said.

At last Catiline appeared alone on the temple steps. The spectators fell silent, amazed at his boldness. But as he strode down the alley of the crowd, they began to growl, then to cry out, and before he reached his bodyguard they were cursing him with all their might, pelting him with eggs, and spitting on him. Yet they did not kill him, for they had heard Cicero's decision. Catiline vanished into a sedan-chair and disappeared down into the streets, making for the city gates.

Then Cicero appeared. If I had thought the cheers were deafening before, they rose even louder and longer now. "Father of Rome," the people cried as he descended, "Father of your Country, Protector of Liberty!" He acknowledged the adulation of the people with a smile, and a wave, but no more, as Tullia and I sat watching. Even she could not believe her eyes; but they were filled with tears.

"Do you understand now, Spurinna?" she said proudly. "Do you see the power of words in Rome? Those with armies and gladiators may be strong. But those who fight with words can never, ever be stopped."

The Unlikely Magician

Unfortunately, my lack of sleep caught up with me on the way back. They carried me, fast asleep, to a guest bedroom in Cicero's house. I remember dreaming that I was trapped in Volturcius' house, with all the conspirators pointing up at me. And then I was flying over the Market like a bird, gazing across the sprawling city.

"Master Spurinna? Please wake up. Sir, please wake up," came the voice of another bird flying beside me, but it was only the steward shaking me awake. He was much more friendly than before, for he was under the impression that my javelin had saved the house he guarded so jealously.

"Yes?" I asked groggily.

"I'm afraid we need you, sir. Very sorry to wake you up, but there is rather an awkward situation in the garden."

I stumbled beside him toward the garden, where I had found Tullia the evening before as she was sitting with Marrucinus and Fulvia. The place was empty now, except for a waiter holding a tray of boiled eggs.

"You woke me up to feed me eggs?"

"No, sir, over there," whispered the steward, pointing to the dense planting of ferns in the far corner. At that moment there came a shout of wild laughter from behind them, and the voice of the philosopher Pantolemos calling, "You there! More, more of those eggs!"

Confused, I picked a couple of eggs off the tray and walked round the clump of ferns. There, to my still greater confusion, sat Pantolemos, who seemed to be drunk; and the man he was slapping on the shoulder affectionately was my own slave, Homer. He seemed to be even more drunk than Pantolemos, and he was busy smashing hardboiled eggs against the elaborate mosaics on the garden floor.

"Homer!" I cried. "What are you doing here? And what on earth is going on?"

"Oh, there, sir, it is you! Very glad you're alive, I may say. Heard all about it, I did, from this gentleman, this learned gentleman here. We are proving the theorems of that great mathematician from Alexandria who – extraordinary insight – look now, if we double the angle . . ."

I saw that they had arranged the eggs into various triangles. No doubt each egg diagram illustrated some profound point of philosophy.

"Homer," I said sternly, "it is clear that you have had too much to drink. There have been complaints. Your philosophy is making a lot of noise, and the steward tells me the kitchen is running out of eggs."

To his credit, Homer was instantly sober, or just about. He and Pantolemos postponed their speculations, and he told me how he had come to be here. It seemed that he had waited in the street outside Volturcius' house for a long time the night before – had even heard the thud in the alley when I fell off the vine – but decided he should report back to Tullia. Then he went to the apartment he had rented, where he fell asleep. When I had not appeared there by noon, he returned to Cicero's house once more, where the only person he could find was Pantolemos. Somehow the servants mistook them for two important Greek philosophers from Athens, perhaps the Consul's guests, and he and Pantolemos had drunk half a big jug of the best wine in Rome. It was at that point, it seemed, that they started calling for hardboiled eggs.

"Well, I'm glad you two are now friends, at least," I replied. "Now tell me, where is Tullia?"

She was, Homer said, in the library with her father, but maybe, he suggested, I would like to put on my toga first? He had carried it halfway across the city for me, after all.

"Quite right," I said, and returned to the guest bedroom where it was lying, neatly folded. Then, looking a little more like a Roman, I headed off toward the library.

Before I got there, however, I heard Tullia's voice floating down the stairs.

"But we can get their names, in writing!" she was saying. "He assured me himself . . ."

"He did not assure *me*," came her father's reply. "Why is that fat man dealing only with you? I'm the Consul, after all."

"He is afraid, Father, that you will blame him and ruin his people."

"I will not," Cicero said. "But you know I cannot act without proof."

"But I can get you just that – eventually!" Tullia answered. "That is what he wants, to deliver the proof through me."

"Through you?" he responded gruffly. "This is no game, daughter. We need hard, tangible proof! Don't forget that half the Judges are Catiline's own brothers-in-law or great-uncles, or heaven knows what. It will take more than a girl's promise to move them to act!"

I was just about to retreat when Cicero hurried out of the library and saw me coming up the stairs. His worried expression lightened somewhat.

"Ah, Spurinna, I am glad to see your face," he said. "Tullia tells me you heard the speech fairly well today."

"Allow me to congratulate you, sir," I answered warmly.

"Thank you, thank you. Yes, it is not every day a Consul is greeted as Father of his Country, it's true. But your congratulations may be somewhat premature. Tullia will tell you, I have no doubt." But then he frowned. "What's all this noise I've been hearing from the garden? They tell me it's a Greek slave of yours."

"He was carried away in a discussion, sir – it's over now, sir," I replied hastily.

"Discussion? Ah, well, the Greeks will do that," Cicero said with a smile. And he excused himself and descended the stairs, chuckling.

I found Tullia inside the library. She was fiddling with a writing tablet.

"Aulus, you're awake!" she smiled.

"Luckily," I said. "I would have missed all the celebrating otherwise."

"Celebrating?" she said. "Oh, the speech, yes."

"Isn't it a great victory?" I said. "Catiline is gone, the conspiracy is finished. We should be celebrating."

She put down the writing tablet and sighed. "Aulus," she said – I noticed that she was calling me 'Aulus' now and not 'Spurinna' – "Aulus, if that's your impression, I'm glad. Not because it's true, but because that's exactly what my father's speech was supposed to make the people think."

"You mean Catiline isn't finished?"

"This is politics, Aulus. If the people thought Catiline had a chance, then we might be in trouble. But he doesn't, because they don't. Do you follow me?

"Of course," I said, lying. "It makes sense. But why *isn't* Catiline finished?"

"Well, to begin with, he's got Manlius and the army in Etruria! That's something. But it's impossible to have a conspiracy of just one person. There have to be other men who are with him, here in Rome. You told me yourself there were two dozen people at Volturcius' house last night."

"But your father knows who they are," I persisted, rattling off some of the names I had heard. "Even that Druid who was here – why can't your father send guards to arrest them?"

"Because, Aulus, you can't just arrest people with no proof!" she said impatiently. "They're not *nobodies*, they have friends, they're Senators and Roman knights. It may even be that Julius Caesar supports them." She sighed again. "No, my father's right, of course. Without proof, our hands are tied. You can't go before the Senate with nothing but . . ." she looked at me blankly ". . . with nothing but a girl's fancy."

"Well," I said, "then we wait. Let's go down to the Market. If you recall, you promised to show me around."

And wait we did – for ten days. Tullia insisted that I sleep in one of the guest bedrooms at Cicero's house, and they found Homer a comfortable spot in the slaves' quarters. She did show me the Market, several times – though mainly, I suspected, in order to have me as an escort while she looked into a hundred shops, for it seemed that Roman ladies were not supposed to stroll around by themselves. I learned a lot about perfume and silk, and Tullia often went to a Celtic merchant who sold beautiful amber gems. But she would not say much about politics. She often disappeared in the evening, sometimes with her friend Fulvia, sometimes alone.

I began to enjoy living in the great city, in spite of its dirt, and its noise, and its peculiar smell. On all sides I heard that things were dull, that commerce was dwindling, and that no one was reveling because of the threat that Catiline still posed. There was a sense of impending danger. Rumors spread that Catiline's friends walked the streets after nightfall, trying to recruit for him. To me the city seemed lively enough during the day, though I did take Tullia's advice to stay inside after supper. Then I labored to amuse myself, usually reading or playing backgammon.

And we did play a lot of backgammon, Homer and I, sitting in the garden on quiet evenings as November wore away. Cicero had no more dinner parties that month, or at least none at his house. We saw him only a few times, still wearing the chain-mail shirt under his Senator's toga. But I enjoyed the backgammon games less than I might have done, for I was thinking more and more about Volturcius, and Homer usually won. Every time he did, he would quote another line from Hesiod.

"At this rate, sir, I shall get through the complete works of that immortal poetic genius," he remarked at one point. "'*These days are blessed for men upon the earth,*' as he so aptly puts it. But perhaps I can interest you in the poems they merely *claim* that he composed?"

So it was with great relief that I saw Tullia and Fulvia approaching us in the garden late one afternoon. I rose to greet them.

"How is the game going?" asked Fulvia. "I hope you are beating the Greeks like a good Roman, Spurinna."

"They must be Greek dice," I said.

"Enough of the game for today," said Tullia. "Aulus, I wish to ask you something. It concerns Volturcius."

"Volturcius?" I put the board away.

"That's right," Tullia said. "I thought you'd be interested. You're still eager to . . ."

"To get him? The murderer?" I cried. Of course I was. I had been thinking of nothing else.

"Good. Well, our plans are coming together again. As you know, Volturcius is a trusted man among these friends of Catiline. They used his house for that meeting. And they have been using him to carry messages between Catiline and Manlius. Fulvia here heard about it."

"How did you hear?" I asked Fulvia. "Surely *you're* not mixed up in this."

"Strange you should ask," Fulvia answered, taking a deep breath. "It was four days ago, when Marrucinus was strolling with me by the theater, and we met our friend who was walking there . . . and she said Volturcius was her husband's Protector here in the city, but he was never home for days on end . . . and her husband had asked all about it, and Volturcius has been traveling, and her husband asked where, and no one would tell him, so he kept asking, and finally they said Faesulae . . . and that's what my friend told me. By the theater. Four days ago." Fulvia stopped long enough to breathe again.

"So you see, Aulus, Volturcius has been to Faesulae since the conspirators had their meeting," continued Tullia. "But Fulvia and I think he's a weak link in their schemes. You see, as everyone knows, he is very superstitious."

"That's true enough," I replied. "You should have seen his study. The little golden dolls, the astrology, the diagrams of animal guts – it was like a temple."

"Right," said Tullia. "He's superstitious. Always wondering what the gods are thinking, the impious brute. His appetite for consultations, for séances and so on, is enormous."

"What does this have to do with avenging my uncle's death?"

"We think we've found a way to crush Volturcius, to trap him and get that proof my father needs. Besides hurting Catiline's cause, that will finish Volturcius, believe me. You see, we know that the conspirators want to bring in Celtic allies . . ."

"I overheard something about that at the meeting. Those 'ten thousand warriors' – that's what you mean?"

"That's it," said Tullia. "But the Celts want proof themselves, proof of good faith, a signed letter from the conspirators asking for their help. Otherwise they won't come."

"A letter? What good is that?"

"It's a sign of trust, Aulus. It would mean they trust the Celts not to betray them. A token."

"Hmm. Alright, but how do you know all this?"

"Patience, Aulus. We've been busy, and we know that much. And we also know that it's Volturcius who is going to deliver the letter!"

"And," interrupted Fulvia, taking another deep breath, "when we heard that, Spurinna, I went back to the theater, not with Marrucinus, and found my friend there. And she and her husband had been to Volturcius' house, just last night . . . for dinner . . . and he was incredibly nervous the whole time! He must be terrified about his mission. He kept asking his guests if they knew any way to make the gods guarantee something important would work – a priest, or a magician, or something. And my friend told me that, and I told her to tell Volturcius there was a wonderful magician in the city who could do anything."

"So," said Tullia smoothly – those two girls were quite a team – "so what do we do? We get you in there to read the letter, and then you swear before my father and the Judges that the letter exists, and then my father can be authorized to seize it! To get the proof, Aulus!"

There was a pause. "And how on earth are you going to get me in to read it?" I asked, dreading the answer, which I knew they must have ready for me.

"Haven't you been paying attention?" asked Tullia. "Obviously, if the man is superstitious, worried about delivering the letter and the mission, we just disguise you as that priest or magician and he'll show it to you, so you can bless it, in the name of the gods. It's all arranged. In fact, you're having dinner there tonight."

"Tonight? Me? Dinner at Volturcius' house? You can't be serious!"

"Fulvia has arranged it, as she always does," Tullia said with a smile. "Isn't that a fine piece of work? You should thank her for it."

"It wasn't easy," Fulvia confirmed. "My friend had to describe your stupendous magic at great length, Spurinna. She said that you're on intimate terms with all the seven planets. And the moon, too."

My mouth fell open. What in heaven's name were these rash young women getting me into? It was madness.

"Now look," I said, recovering. "In all reason, how is Volturcius going to believe I have this stupendous magical knack when I'm not even twenty years old?" Another pause. The girls bit their lips. "I've seen pictures of these fortune-tellers," I went on, seizing my advantage, "I even saw a couple of them in the Market yesterday. They're all at least sixty years old! They're from some place out East you've never heard of! They've got beards as long as my arm! They do *not*," I concluded, "look like respectable young Roman citizens. Like me," I added, for emphasis.

Now Tullia and her friend looked positively discouraged, and I almost felt sorry for the failure of their scheme.

Meanwhile, Homer had been sitting beside me the whole time, playing idly with the backgammon dice. But when he heard me describe myself as a respectable young Roman citizen, he couldn't help coughing heavily. That cough was his undoing.

Tullia's eyes lit up. "Steward!" she called. "Yes, steward, bring me the holiday beard, it's in the small storeroom. Here," she said, when the steward returned with a dusty gray false beard, which did look suitable for a carnival. It hooked on behind the ears, with no moustache. "Here it is," she said.

I backed firmly away. "Nothing will convince me . . ." I began.

"Not you, Aulus. You there, philosopher, stand up a moment." She gestured to Homer. "Try this on." Homer glanced at me in terror, but obeyed. "Yes," said Tullia with delight. "Yes, oh yes, that's it! If we just add a bright red shirt . . . no, embroidered, with strange signs . . . and a staff . . . no, a wand . . . and a hat, a floppy felt hat. Where will we find that, I wonder? Steward, send down to the Market and buy a fortune-teller's clothes. The price doesn't matter. And send for my seamstress."

If it were not for the fact that two pretty girls were gazing at him with admiration, I think Homer would have torn the beard off at this point and run screaming from the garden. He had heard the whole conversation, of course, and he knew as well as I did they were going to dress him up like a sorcerer and send him straight into the lion's den.

"You know," I said carefully, "I think this just might work."

"Sir, please," said Homer, turning to me. "I understand what is happening here, and I beg you, sir, I entreat you, do not dress me up as a carnival attraction! I am a student of the Muses, sir, and your humble secretary, not some . . ."

"Yes indeed," I said to Tullia. "A stroke of genius. He's perfect."

Homer was still sulking heavily by the time the slave returned from the Market, with a set of robes so exotic they were one great heap of purple. But Tullia took so much pleasure in helping him into them, adjusting his beard, and teaching him how to wave his wand that he only scratched the back of his head under his floppy felt hat and complained that he didn't know anything about sorcery.

"That doesn't matter, Homer," I informed him. "Dress makes the man. You look splendid, a genuine magician."

"And speaking of genuine," Tullia said, "we just have time to decide what we should wear."

"We?"

"You and I, Aulus. We're going to be the magician's assistants, his slaves, at Volturcius' house. The whole idea is to allow you to read that letter, remember?" She gave Homer an affectionate hug. "Surely you don't think a magician this splendid would perform all by himself?"

9

Trickery and Treason

As Tullia, Homer, and I were carried in Fulvia's sedan-chair to the house of Volturcius, I was filled with anxiety. We looked a strange crew by now: Homer in his get-up, and Tullia and I both wearing ribboned shirts and copious amounts of make-up. I had never seen her happier than when she applied the paint to my eyelids. But in the end we did look exotic, so I suppose it was worth it.

If anything, Homer was more nervous than I was. He spent the whole ride running over some "magical" phrases he had once heard, and trying to get his astrological signs straight. "The Scales, yes," he muttered, "and then the Scorpion. Also the Goat – or is it the Deer? Sir, I'll never remember this nonsense!"

"Don't fret," Tullia soothed him. "You'll do fine, Homer. Just be careful that you don't call Aulus 'Sir,' alright? And don't call me 'Madam.' And you, Aulus, if you have to speak to him, he's 'Master' or 'My Lord.' But neither you nor I should speak at all if we can help it."

"I won't say anything," I assured her, "especially if it means calling my own slave 'My Lord.'"

Soon – far too soon – we reached Volturcius' front door in Sicklemaker Street. The bearers set the sedan-chair down, and we got out to find two torches blazing by the silent iron doors. There were no guards to be seen. The sedan-chair left us.

As Homer's "assistant," I knocked boldly three times, and immediately the door swung open. In the light of the torches, little could be seen inside.

"Greetings, most venerable Narmer," for that was the name Fulvia's friend had chosen for her imaginary magician when she had arranged the invitation. "I am pleased that you have come," the quiet rasping voice continued. "You are welcome, in the name of all the gods."

It was Volturcius. He seemed to be alone. Homer stepped gravely forward, and we followed him.

The hall was rather cleaner, tidier, and more richly decorated than I had expected, for I had seen only the messy study and the dismal kitchen corridor before. Glints of gold gleamed from the paintings, which depicted obscure Eastern myths. Incense floated in the air. And in the middle of the hall I at last laid eyes on my uncle's killer.

He was a thin man, older than Homer had described him. One felt that he was naturally shy; but there was an eagerness to his bows and the swing of his arm as he greeted Homer – "the friend of the planets," he called him.

And behind that eagerness I sensed a hidden cruelty, a
secret pleasure in the frailty of human life. Remembering
our purpose there, I suppressed an urge to kick him.

As Volturcius led us toward the dining hall, we passed
the ball court on our left – from the other side. It was dark
and smelled dusty. Perhaps no one had played there since
the conspirators' secret meeting. Indeed, the house seemed
empty as Tullia and I marching meekly behind Homer's
trailing robes.

The absence of slaves was peculiar in a rich house, the
more so since I knew Volturcius owned many of them. But
far more startling was the presence of Volturcius' one guest
that evening. We found him lying on a couch beside the
dinner table, humming gently, and helping himself to
grapes. With an icy chill of terror, I recognized the red hair
and beard, the colorfully patterned toga, and the blue
tattoo that was sketched on his cheek. It was the Druid I had
seen at Cicero's table, whose singsong accent I had heard
among Catiline's most trusted associates, the man who had
promised them 'ten thousand warriors' that night.

Volturcius introduced him as a Celtic ambassador from
the north of Italy – quite correct, as far as it went. Homer
reclined on the couch facing him, Volturcius between
them, and Tullia and I took our places cross-legged on the
floor between Homer's couch and the table. It felt awkward
down there, where the slaves were supposed to sit. I could

hardly believe I was Homer's 'slave' that evening. Also, I was worried. I hung my head as low as I dared, for surely the Druid would recognize us, make-up or no make-up. Hadn't he chatted with Tullia before? I could feel his gaze on me – a penetrating gaze, far more intelligent than Volturcius'. Moreover, the man was a sorcerer, and surely he would notice Homer's total incompetence at magic.

Dinner was served, carried in by a single waiter. Oysters to start with, in the Thracian style, and then roast rabbit with a heavy fish sauce, and then grilled turbot. Volturcius ate greedily, stuffing the oysters one by one into his mouth and wiping the sauce on his napkin. The Druid also liked to eat. But Homer refused everything, though he did pass food down to us where we sat on the floor. That night his "slaves" dined rather well; the truth is, he hated oysters.

"Forgive, most honored lord, my refusal of this feast," he said to Volturcius. "But it is quite impossible. The action of the stomach, you see, has a bad effect upon the magic powers. Indeed," he continued, "I may tell you that I have not touched food, nor tasted so much as water, for seven full days. For I value the truth, honored lord, and I prize the truth that we shall determine here tonight."

Of course, Homer had been drinking Cicero's best wine for seven full days, but Volturcius didn't know that, and he was exceedingly impressed. Clearly he could not imagine a human being rejecting fine food, and he seemed to think it was a sign of Homer's special understanding with the gods. I began to wonder if Homer might actually pull this off.

When dessert came, Homer kept bluffing. "The honeyed pears are delicious, I have no doubt," he said. "But, lord, the planets are aligning as we speak, and I am a busy man, sir, a very busy man. There is a great demand for my wisdom in the city. Julius Caesar himself has been known to seek my wisdom."

"Venerable Narmer, I have heard of your powers, your wonders," said Volturcius. "I am told that you know all the secret symbols of the East."

"Of the East, the South, the North, and also the West!" said Homer sternly. "And also somewhat of the South-East. For sixty years, my lord, I have delved into such matters. That is the secret of my remarkably youthful appearance," he added. "But I have never found more divine knowledge than when I served with the Priests of Ra in Egypt. Except, of course, in the poems of Hesiod."

"Hesiod!" exclaimed Volturcius. "That old Greek poet? I always thought he was very boring."

"Hesiod, my lord, boring? Hesiod, boring!" Homer lifted both hands towards the ceiling. "By the seven waters of Tigris," he exclaimed, "even I can only guess the depth of his divine insight. Though admittedly," he added, "it is rare in this fallen age to meet anyone who can perceive it."

"It is fascinating, venerable Narmer. Fascinating. I would never have suspected! Yet perhaps we should, with your blessing, proceed with your séance?"

"Yes, we must do so, immediately."

The waiter hastily cleared the table and withdrew. I peered at the Druid from my station, but he was merely staring curiously at the venerable Narmer. Certainly he did not know who I was, and he did not seem to notice Tullia. But I trembled to think of his professional opinion of a séance led by Homer.

"First, Volturcius," said my slave, "you must state the subject on which you wish to consult the spirit world."

"I . . . I will state it," answered the murderer with some hesitation. "It concerns an enterprise, undertaken by myself and my friends. We have had some setbacks. The chief man in the enterprise has left, but we hope he will return soon, and then we will succeed. But he faces great challenges, and to assist him we hope certain other friends of ours" – he gave a nod to the Druid – "will come to our aid. And it falls to me to convince them to bring us that aid. I am going to ride, if the omens favor it, with a message for them . . . a letter, for these new friends. A guarantee," he ended.

"Very well," said Homer. "The subject has been stated." He fished around in his robes for a pouch of leather, from which he produced the backgammon dice we had been using. He gave them a lucky squeeze. "Now, my lord, what do you wish to know?"

"Whether our enterprise will succeed!" blurted out Volturcius. He was shaking with excitement. "And also, will the guarantee work? Will it convince our friends?"

"Have you any astrological charts in the house?" asked Homer. "We must determine which of the gods we should consult."

Volturcius did indeed have charts, as I knew well. He sent the waiter up to his study, and the man returned with a sheaf of different charts under his arm, which he placed on the table in front of Homer's couch.

"Hmm, yes," said Homer judiciously, looking through them. "Quite a variety, I see. Quite a mixed lot. Look, this one is most inaccurate, and this one is quite outdated."

"Outdated?"

"Yes. I mean, not outdated, but innovative, far too innovative. What times we live in! But this one here will do well." He chose a brightly colored chart. "My assistant will roll the dice. No, not the boy, the girl. An unlucky lad, when it comes to these dice," he explained to Volturcius.

Tullia took the dice and rolled them, with a graceful toss, over the chart.

"Let me see, let me see," Homer mused, peering down. "Yes, as I suspected, it is Saturn who will reveal your fate. Saturn, the Father of the King of the Gods, the ten times venerable Son of the Sky, the Overthrown and Overthrower, who:

Worked never deed of violence, nor stole
Whatever 'neath the Titans was her role."

Those lines at least I recognized. Homer often quoted them. I looked over at Tullia, who was frowning, but Volturcius was too entranced to notice that Hesiod had been dragged in again.

"Yes, Saturn!" he exclaimed, repeating all of the titles Homer had provided, and even the quotation.

"Now we must have the letter, the guarantee," Homer declared with confidence. "My other assistant will read it aloud to the heavenly spirits."

There was a pause.

"The letter?" asked Volturcius. "Must you touch it?" He looked over at the Druid, frowning. The Druid frowned back. "I have not even let my friend here touch it," Volturcius explained. "You see, venerable Narmer, I have sworn it will not leave my grasp. I have sworn!" He produced it from the inside of his toga – a large, expensive papyrus sheet. But he could not bring himself to part with it just yet.

"Ah, yes, you have sworn," said Homer. "But have we not all sworn oaths, in the folly of youth? When I was young, Volturcius – but that was long ago – I worried about such things. Yes, indeed I did, for days on end. But do not forget that we must also obey the will of heaven! And if the gods will help you, they must know your aim. They must hear your letter!"

Another pause followed. Volturcius was struggling with himself. At last, with great reluctance, his hand reached across the table and deposited the letter in my lap. I heard him mutter, "Overthrower and Overthrown" in despair.

"Excellent, we are making progress," said Homer, as much to me as to Volturcius. "Now read, slave."

I read out the letter in a clear voice. It ran as follows:

"We, the undersigned, do hereby swear eternal and everlasting friendship with the Celtic tribe of the Allobroges.

We do so with the understanding that they shall bring to our assistance, as loyal allies, ten thousand warriors of foot and eight hundred of horse soldiers, who will combine with the army of the Consul of Rome, Catiline, to overthrow the illegitimate and tyrannical power now in possession of the city; and the Celtic soldiers will take the field no later than the last day of November.

For our part, we swear, by all the gods, and by Jupiter especially, king of the gods, the following:

First, the Celtic soldiers shall have their own commanders.

Second, any money or property taken from the city shall be divided fairly between Romans and Celts.

Third, the lands inhabited by the Celtic tribe of the Allobroges shall be theirs, and theirs alone, for all the generations to come, and shall not be subject to Roman tax-gatherers, and they shall never have to worship any gods except their own."

The letter itself looked most impressive: it was no ordinary document. The sheet had been scraped with pumice stone, and the edges marked neatly with expensive purple dye: a letter not so much to be read as to be treasured. At the bottom were twenty signatures and personal seals in wax. My hand was shaking by the time I read out the last Senator's name: I was holding in my hand the ultimate proof of Catiline's conspiracy.

Homer, however, had begun to sing softly as I read the document. Now his voice swelled to a chant; but he was chanting total gibberish. I don't think he knew himself what language it was supposed to be. It was almost hypnotic. At last he gave three throaty cries and shouted, "If you disapprove of this venture, O Saturn, then show us a sign!"

We all tensed; but absolutely nothing happened.

"It is done!" Homer shouted again, with evident relief. "The mighty Saturn, Overthrower and Overthrown, approves of your plan entirely!"

"He does?" cried Volturcius. "He likes the plan? But . . . but what of the timing? Does he approve the timing?"

"What's that?" asked Homer.

"The timing, venerable Narmer. When should I go? I am supposed to leave with the Celts tomorrow evening!"

Homer seemed at a loss, as though his bag of tricks were empty at last. But he recovered.

"I am afraid the, ah, *timing*, as you put it, or any question of time, cannot be determined, not without consulting the liver of a black sheep. A black *male* sheep," he threw in, for good measure.

My heart sank.

"I have just the thing on hand!" cried Volturcius. He called for the waiter. "Waiter, tell the guards to fetch the black ram from the stable. The *healthy* one," he added in an undertone. "And don't forget the sacrificial knife."

I glanced at Homer. He darted a look of utter hopelessness at me. But we had both heard the word *guards* and realized we were now committed to sacrificing a sheep.

"Wonderful, wonderful," Homer announced, when the poor beast was led in. It looked heavily drugged. "My assistant will slaughter it, and I will read the liver." He gave me a sharp kick in the ribs with his foot.

Now, I had seen ceremonies like this before, though I had never conducted a sacrifice. I felt sorry for the black sheep as the guards, wearing chain-mail shirts and carrying daggers, now shoved it toward me. Taking the sacrificial knife, I gave the beast a merciful blow on the head with the hilt, knocking it unconscious, and then I took its life.

Blood poured everywhere, across the table, the cushions, and Homer's couch. My ribboned shirt was stained bright red. I saw a cruel gleam in Volturcius eye: he seemed to be enjoying the procedure. The Druid was pale with anxiety. He snatched the precious letter from the table just in time, before the blood could reach it.

Now an even uglier moment was coming, for Homer had to open the beast's belly. More blood, unfortunately; and then, dipping his hand into the guts, he pulled out something.

"Aha," he said. "If I judge correctly – and I have never been wrong – tomorrow evening is perfect for you, my lord. The gods . . ."

"But that is not the liver!" cried Volturcius. "You must know, Narmer, you are holding the pancreas."

"Hm, yes, I see you understood my joke," laughed Homer. "The pancreas indeed. Your piety is to be commended. But here" – and he reached in again with a look of disgust – "here we have the correct token. And, let me see, no, it seems you must postpone, sir. You must postpone your journey . . ."

Even I could tell he had not found the liver. He was holding a piece of intestine.

"That is not the liver either!" cried Volturcius, rising. "What on earth are you doing, venerable Narmer? Have you forgotten your skills?"

"Do you presume to tell me my profession?" shouted Homer. His pent-up rage at my uncle's murderer was suddenly surfacing. And it was, perhaps, his only choice under the circumstances. "Do you, a mere mortal, dare to argue with the venerable Narmer? Will you insult the celestial powers? By the five – no, the seven – waters of Tigris, Volturcius, you have behaved badly! Very badly!"

But they were staring at him with disbelief. Tullia and I leapt instantly to our feet. For in his rage Homer's floppy hat had fallen off, and his beard was attached to just one ear – it was dangling to the right, exposing his chin.

Volturcius shot him a shocked, horrified look that turned immediately to overpowering fury.

"Guards!" he called. "Guards, seize him! Seize him!"

Everyone moved at once. Tullia jumped over the couch, grabbing Homer by the neck, and they raced for the front door with Volturcius at their heels. He was in a frightening rage, screaming for "the head of the imposter, the head of the defiler! Bring me his head, do you hear me?"

I could not follow them: I slipped in the pool of blood. The sacrificial knife went flying. But the guards were only concerned with Homer, so I was able to pick myself up and scramble deeper into the house.

I had not gone five paces, however, when I realized the Druid was behind me.

"Stop, boy! Stop now!" came his singsong voice. The rest was in Celtic. I guessed they were powerful curses, invoked upon my head in the name of his foreign gods.

I rounded a corner at top speed, but saw I was only heading to the garden. Wheeling back, I almost collided with the great bulk of the tall Druid, who was coming straight for me. His hand snatched at the neck of my shirt, but I dodged it. Out of the corner of my eye I saw he still had the document, the letter, in his hand, but I did not pause to try to snatch it from his mighty grip.

The corridor was pitch black, but I ran on. Then there was cool air on my left: I could see a short flight of stairs. I was down them before the Druid reached the top. I took the stairs three at a time.

Now I followed the passage below, around another corner, slipping but catching myself. In front of me, the passage looked oddly familiar. Of course, I realized, the kitchen corridor! And the door at the end could only be the low doorway to the alley. Down the whole length of the passage I built up speed, hurling myself against the door, leaving the ground as I struck it with my shoulder. It flew open, and I flew out behind it, landing in the very same pile of scraps that had broken my fall before.

But I heard the Druid following, charging down the passage.

"Stop there, boy! Where do you think you are going?" he called, but I was already up and running fast, back towards Sicklemaker Street and the glow of the torches. Homer and Tullia had gone that way.

I reached the street. Behind me came the voice of the Druid, filled with despair – or was it one last prayer to the gods to smite me? I turned and saw his shape silhouetted by the moonlight, arms raised up to heaven, beard shaking.

I turned to Sicklemaker Street. Where were they? Even as I asked myself the question, I saw them not far down the street. Two guards were chasing them, Homer was tripping over his magic robes, and Tullia was almost dragging him along. I flew after them.

The first guard snarled, nearly on them. But the guards were too intent on catching Homer to see me coming up behind. With a single sweep of my leg I caught their heels, sending them sprawling into the mud of the street.

"Now come on!" I cried, helping Tullia with Homer. "Down here, the way we took when we arrived before. You remember, Homer?"

It was only a little street, but it went the right way. On we ran, to exhaustion, until we deliberately lost our way and our pursuers with it. When we could hear them no more, we stopped to catch our breath.

"Well, that was lucky," I gasped after a while. "A black sheep! A black *male* sheep! Why didn't you just say no?"

"Easy enough for you, sir, if I may say!" answered Homer, breathing hard. "Sitting there the whole time while

I had to talk! How was I supposed to know he had a black male sheep – and in the house, ready for us? Besides, I studied philosophy, sir, not anatomy!"

"That's enough arguing," said Tullia. "Homer, you did splendidly. And you're quite right, Aulus, it *was* lucky. Because, in the end, we did it! You read the letter, didn't you? My plan worked! We know everything. And now there is not a moment to lose!"

In the Hall of Justice

I decided the next morning that I would never again be chased through Volturcius' house. Or chased at all, for that matter. My shoulder was bruised where I had slammed into the door, and my muscles ached. But I felt better when I found Homer in the garden, and I promised to buy him a new set of dice for the backgammon, to replace his lost pair. I told him he had done very well indeed – splendidly, in fact.

"I would never have thought you had it in you, Homer," I said. "When you were chanting that gibberish, I nearly mistook you for a real magician."

"It wasn't bad, sir, if I do say so myself. Convincing, anyway. And I did manage to get in a good word about Hesiod, did you notice? Even if it was to Volturcius." He spat.

"It's strange that we've looked him in the face. Volturcius, I mean. Can you believe he murdered my uncle?"

"Yes, sir, I can. You should have seen him when you killed the sheep. He would have liked it even more if you hadn't

114

knocked it unconscious first, in my opinion. An evil man, sir, a very evil man. But we shall get him yet, won't we?"

We shook hands on that idea, but just then Tullia joined us and said I had to go.

"My father will be ready shortly," she said, "and the sedan-chair is waiting. Aulus, what's wrong with your toga? I told you, you must keep your elbow firm against your side or it starts to slip. There," she said, with a last dusting of my arm, "that will do. You could be a Senator's son."

Tullia was almost as eager as I was, though without my nervousness. I was about to be taken to a meeting of the Judges of Rome, and her plan to retrieve the proof we had seen last night depended on my testimony. Neither of us had gotten much sleep, for we had awakened her father in the middle of the night to describe everything to him. Then Cicero had grilled me for confirmation. Now it was the first hour after dawn, but she could at least go back to bed.

I waited by the sedan-chair, and Cicero soon appeared. Bowing, I climbed in after him. By now I was getting used to this way of traveling, the gliding on the flat stretches interrupted by those sickening lurches, the people staring in as you went by, the steady rhythm of the bearers' marching feet. Cicero took it all for granted; and he had other things on his mind.

"I hope this charade with Volturcius seems as rash and ill-considered to you as it does to me," he said. "It is not a good policy for young people to throw themselves like this into the line of battle, without asking the opinion of the Consul in the next room. Still," he frowned, "it will indeed be a remarkable stroke if we can bring it off. It was my daughter's idea, I presume?"

"Yes, sir, entirely," I said. "Though I saw the possibilities right away," I added.

"Yes. Hmm. Incidentally, Tullia has asked me to tell you not to make any mention at this meeting with the Judges, of this Celt, this Druid, whom you saw last night. You will refrain from doing so?"

"Of course, sir, if you say so," I replied. "But why?"

He sighed in response. "My daughter has her reasons for it. Young man, if I did not foresee that you will have many daughters, I would suggest that you not have any. Or at least," he corrected himself, "I suggest that you do not allow them to read legends of the heroic women of the ancient Romans when they are children, followed by complicated political biographies when they are older. It can have a strange effect."

"Not even your own biography, sir? I can't imagine how *that* could harm a girl."

He looked at me and chuckled. "Well, you have me there. Perhaps *you* can read it to your daughter, seeing as you are taking a large part in it these days."

We arrived at the law courts, just behind the Roman Market, and got out. Following a step behind the Consul, surrounded by his bodyguard of ax-men, I marveled at the tall pillars of the Hall of Justice, whose front steps we ascended. The bailiffs there saluted as we passed into the cool shade inside. All was deserted now, for it was one of the officially Unlucky Days, when no case was tried or lawsuit pleaded. I saw the marble jury seats, the Judge's high chair, the witness platform, and the benches for the accused and his family. Many Senators, innocent and guilty, had sat on those benches over the centuries. Now it was strangely quiet. But we went through this hall to a room behind it, low and long, lit by sunlight filtering in from small, square windows above our heads.

Six Judges sat there, on stools behind a polished wooden table. They were all Senators, and they ranked only one degree beneath the two Consuls. Though one of them was too old to be ambitious, the rest were no doubt eager to be elected as Consuls themselves before long. I noticed the tall man I had seen from a distance once before: Julius Caesar. He was courteous, but no more than that, when Cicero walked in, and he followed the proceedings with the most intelligent expression I have ever seen.

"It is my pleasure, gentlemen, on this important occasion, to introduce this young man," began Cicero. "His family and mine have been friends for many generations, and for ten years now they have been under my Protection. This is Aulus Lucinus Spurinna, from Etruria. Some of you knew his grandfather, I believe, also of that name."

"Welcome, Aulus Lucinus," said the Chief Judge. "We understand that we have been called here by the Consul because you possess information concerning Catiline and the safety of the Republic. Please provide it."

I swallowed the sharp stabs of fear, and provided it.

"Yesterday evening," I said, "I was a guest of Volturcius, a Roman knight, whom some of you may know. He owns land near Faesulae in my country, and he was acquainted with my uncle. It was not known to Volturcius, however, that I was present. I was there because of a private quarrel between the man and my family, and for the occasion, my slave and myself . . ." I left out Tullia ". . . had disguised ourselves as . . . uh, well . . . as magicians from the East. That part is complicated," I added apologetically. "But in the course of the evening I was shown a letter that was signed by twenty Romans, some of them Senators and the rest Roman knights." And here I repeated the letter exactly, word for word, and added the names I had seen at the bottom. "Each signature had a wax seal from a personal ring beside it," I concluded, "and the papyrus was of the very best quality."

There I ended. As each of the names had come out – and I allowed each name to resonate in that low room before adding the next – there was an intake of breath from the Judges. Some of the names brought low mutters. By the end there was a look of consternation on their faces, but, I saw with relief, no sign of doubt. The oldest Senator did interrupt to comment that a Roman citizen dressing up as a magician from the East, that such a thing could not have happened in his day, it was quite unheard of. But the Judges were clearly appalled at the possibility that the Allobroges tribe would come down to assist Catiline with those 'ten thousand warriors.'

"This is what comes of delaying their lawsuit these last five years," commented one.

"But what now?" was the universal question. "If Catiline can control them . . ."

"Where is Volturcius now?" asked Caesar.

"If I may speak, gentlemen," said Cicero, "I will tell you that I have a plan for dealing with the situation. Volturcius is in the city, but we do not know where exactly. We searched his house before dawn, but the letter was not there, and undoubtedly he has it with him. He cannot destroy it, for as proof of good faith to the tribe, it is essential to Catiline's conspiracy. No, he will try to deliver it, for though he may have been imposed upon with, ah, with false magicians, he does not know we are aware of his design. Moreover, thanks to our young friend here, we know that he plans to ride this very night, and so he must. As you know, my colleague Antonius will soon march against Manlius with our army, and Catiline needs those Celts."

He paused, and the Judges sat on the edge of their seats.

"Gentlemen, there is only one road to Manlius' camp, to Catiline, and from there to the north and to the Celtic tribe. The Cassian Road from the Mulvian Bridge. That is the road Volturcius must take. It is therefore my opinion that we must dispatch riders – a strong force of riders – to seize Volturcius and his most treasonous letter. I suggest that they catch him at the Mulvian Bridge. Two troops of cavalry should suffice."

The Judges were delighted with this plan, or perhaps that there was any plan at all, and they gave it their hearty approval. Two of them suggested men to lead the cavalry: their own nephews, by coincidence.

"That will do well," said Cicero. "I am glad we are all agreed. But if I may make another suggestion, I would add that young Spurinna here should accompany our force. He can identify the document in question."

"He seems like a capable young man," said Caesar.

"Good. And, gentlemen, since this time of danger for the Republic is one in which we recognize our friends – like we recognize our enemies – more clearly, I hope we may all join in affirming that without such loyal allies as this young citizen here, allies from the regions of Italy on which the strength of this city in large measure depends, we would be in still greater danger than we now are; and, therefore, as a measure of our gratitude . . ."

Cicero was not looking at me as he said this, but the Judges were; and I saw they were annoyed. Certainly Cicero was about to ask one of them to take me on as part of an entourage, perhaps for a share in the rich provinces each of them would shortly go to govern. I would become some-body's burden, a burden they could not refuse. My own spirits slumped at the idea. More than ever, I wished I were back in my own house, even with my schoolwork, without powerful people staring at me, without the prospect of being dragged out East to tackle a life I knew nothing about. But it looked like I would shortly be trapped into doing just that.

". . . of our gratitude and appreciation," continued Cicero. "Now then, it has come to my attention that the house of Spurinna is being menaced by threats to their land. Though they are in the right, the lawsuit that would result from these troubles would nevertheless be extensive and expensive. No doubt it would eventually end up before you gentlemen as Judges. Therefore it is my hope that you will agree to sign with me, here and now, this document." He produced a scroll from the pouch of his toga. "This document, gentlemen, guarantees the right of Spurinna and his tenants to their land, and also the Protection, the special Protection of that right, from the Senate and the Roman People forever. May I have the pen?"

The Judges' faces lightened. It was nothing, after all, just a land dispute, and they were happy to sign it. Within moments, as it seemed to me, the document bore their seals and signatures, and Julius Caesar himself put it into my hand.

"It's heartening to think," he said, "that there are still Protectors in Italy whose first thought is for their people."

For my part, I did think of the tenants, and how happy they would be to see this, even if they could not read it. Aunt Hercna would be happy too. And then I thought of our old house, small enough compared to the great Roman Hall of Justice. But it was my home, and I remembered our own front hall there and my grandfather's statue beside the door. And then I had to fight an urge to laugh, for as I pictured that statue now, in my mind's eye, it was smiling.

In the sedan-chair on our way back, Cicero did not say much. He was preoccupied with papers. I heard something about "the wretched grain supply," and I left him to it, happily gazing out the window, lost in my own thoughts. But as we began to climb the hill on which his house stood, he put down his work and spoke to me.

"No doubt you're wondering why I'm sending you with the cavalry tonight. It's not because you can spot a document better than the next man," he said wryly. "No. The fact of the matter is that, though her name did not come up – you have my thanks for that, incidentally – Tullia is going to go along as well, strange as that may sound. And you are going to look after her." He raised his eyebrows. "You understand me on that? You will only be an acting officer, of course, and that merely for form's sake. But you will have two or three riders under your command, and you are going to use them to see that my daughter comes to no harm whatsoever. Also," he added, "that she does not put herself in the front of the battle, if there is one. Is that understood?"

"Yes, sir," I said. "I will make sure of it."

We got out at his front door. "I'm glad you have that document from the Judges," he added. "A useful thing. I will have my scribes make copies for you, and we will put one in the city records. While they are doing that, you may see the guards for a helmet and chain-mail, and a cavalry cloak."

"Thank you, sir, very much, for all you've done," I said. "But may I ask if your scribes are very busy?"

"Busy?" he asked. "I suppose not. Why?"

"Well, sir, if they're available, I have one last favor to ask of you."

11

Encounter at the Bridge

Homer's donkey had been well cared for during our stay at Cicero's house. In fact, the beast was getting fat, and Homer was headed in that direction himself. When he mounted up, both the donkey and the Greek gave a groan. I mounted my white mare, now wearing a fine red cloak (somewhat too big), a helmet, and chain-mail (just the right size). Tullia wore a veil, a deep green traveling cloak, and a wool dress. She was already in the saddle, waiting for us, and looking, to my annoyance, every inch the able rider.

It was approaching noon, the time when the crowds thinned as most pedestrians sought shelter from the sun. The three of us rode down to the Field of Mars, to the north of the Market, where we were to meet the troops of cavalry and ride to the Mulvian Bridge. Volturcius and the Celts, we thought, would not ride 'til the evening, but we were going to leave the city by the southern gate, taking the long way round to the bridge to avoid comment.

And it was indeed a fine force that accompanied us. We saw the glint of them a long way off: fifty riders in their best armor, drawn up in rows beside their horses on the grassy meadow. When we approached they thumped the ends of their spears on the ground in greeting.

Two officers sat on their steeds in front: the Judges' nephews. The larger one, a burly young man with a golden clasp on his cloak, saluted and called to Tullia.

"Madam," he said, "my name is Flaccus. We are at the Consul's disposal. My colleague's name is Pomptinus." He gestured at the other officer, who gave us a leer and took a swig from the fat drinking-bladder in his other hand. "Please forgive my colleague's thirst," said Flaccus with some embarrassment. "The heat of the day, you understand. You are Spurinna, right? Very good. These are the men you are to command. Always glad to meet a friend of Cicero. And to see you, madam," he added with a grin. "You may not remember me, but I met you when you were about seven years old."

"Of course I remember, Flaccus," replied Tullia. "You were about fifteen, and you broke my father's Athenian vase with your slingshot."

"Yes, hmm. That may be. But I've traded in the slingshot since then," he answered easily. "Traded it for this troop of riders. The best in Rome. No need to fear the Celts today." Then, more seriously, in a low voice: "We are to ride to the Mulvian Bridge, right? But we leave by the southern gate?"

"Just so," said Tullia. "And your men are not to make a racket or show off to the crowd. I will tell you more when we reach the bridge."

"Very good, madam," replied the officer, and he told the trumpeter to blow the signal to move out.

Move out we did, discreetly. The sergeant knew his business, and even if Pomptinus was incompetent (which no one seemed to doubt), Flaccus seemed fearless. Five cavalrymen were under my command, three riding in front of Tullia, Homer, and myself, and two behind. We kept in the middle of the column as it snaked its way around the Market to the southern gate, from which the road led down to the sea.

At first I wondered if it was worth going so far out of our way. But though the cavalry kept to itself, it still excited much comment among the people; and just as Tullia had hoped, the rumors in the street did not connect us to the Mulvian Bridge.

"They're reinforcements for the East, if you must know," said one man in a sausage shop to his friend. "A fine lot."

"But who's the lady there, with the veil?" asked his companion.

"Why, that's the Governor's young wife, of course. Ready for a long sea voyage, ma'am?" he called, making Tullia laugh.

Soon we left the city behind and passed into the countryside. Wide estates stretched on both sides of the road, with slaves working their fields, and here and there an old-fashioned village. In due course we cut to the right and made for the Tiber river. The afternoon was wearing out as we crossed a deep ford, the water coming up to our ankles. Homer shivered on the smaller donkey as the current rose to his knees.

"Sir, I regret anything I may have said against that bridge we crossed when we first got here. By heaven, sir, I'm freezing! You would think it was the primitive water of Ocean, which, as Hesiod says,

> *Is famed for chill, and from its lofty fount*
> *Flows 'neath the earth beneath the jagged mount*

And believe me, sir, I'm not exaggerating!"

Reaching the far bank, we pressed on. Still, what with the bright sun and the cold river, several riders were falling behind the column. Flaccus grew frustrated at this, feeling it disgraced the troop, and he excused himself and rode back angrily. But in his haste he spurred his horse across the rocks beside the road, and the animal screamed as it planted its hoof on a razor-sharp stone. We spun round and saw Flaccus hit the road with a crack, hurled from the saddle through the air with tremendous force.

"Pomptinus!" Tullia cried, turning back to where Flaccus lay, unconscious and bleeding from his scalp. The cavalrymen supported him, washing the wound with water from their flasks, but it was no use. They slung him unceremoniously across his horse. We had to leave him at the next village, to be cared for by his servant, for he already had developed a fever. Unfortunately Pomptinus was now in command.

He spent more time squeezing his drinking-bladder for the last drop of wine, however, than he did in giving orders. Then he stopped at an inn to buy more, while the whole troop waited. Tullia rode beside him after that, all but begging him to hurry. "It is absolutely essential, Pomptinus . . . are you listening, Pomptinus? Listen, I say! We *must* reach the bridge before dark, we simply must!"

Gradually, the officer sagged in the saddle. He dropped the empty drinking-bladder, his head drooped, and he fell fast asleep. The old cavalry sergeant glanced at him with profound disgust.

"Disgraceful is what I call it. If that's a Roman noble, I'm a Greek." He cleared his throat noisily. "Now then, one officer left," he added, smiling at me toothlessly. "What say you, sir?"

"What do you mean?" I asked.

"He means you're in command," said Tullia. "And I must tell you, Aulus, that we still have four miles to go, and these fifty men are far too slow! Order them to hurry, please."

I turned to the trumpeter. "Give whatever signal means 'hurry,'" I said.

The trumpeter looked at the sergeant, but the old man said something nasty and the signal sounded. At once the riders reformed, and we picked up our pace as the sun dropped towards the horizon. I rode in front with the sergeant, peering through the falling dark.

At last we reached the paved surface of the Cassian Road and trotted briskly back in the direction of the river and the city. The Mulvian Bridge was not far off. I saw that it was wider than I had expected, though in need of repair. The Tiber rushed swiftly beneath its three brown arches. Two peasants, who had been fishing from the closest arch, took to their heels when they saw us riding in, but I sent my five men to bring them back, and when I questioned them they swore no one had crossed the bridge that evening. So we were not too late.

"Sergeant," I said, "a Roman knight will be riding this way sometime tonight. Our mission is to arrest him on the bridge."

"Very good, sir."

"He will have a bodyguard of Celts with him, but we will not be the first ones to attack," I went on. "My plan is to divide our force in half and take them from both sides when they cross. I will cross the river with twenty-five riders, and we will hide behind the low ridge there. You stay on this side with the other twenty-five. When the enemy is on the bridge, you will block them in front and I will come up behind and capture the knight. We didn't leave the city from this road, so they won't be expecting us. Any questions?"

"No, sir. But what about this . . . uh, this officer?" he asked, indicating Pomptinus, who had begun to snore loudly.

"Keep him on your side, in the bushes. And keep out of sight yourselves until you hear the signal: three notes on the trumpet."

"Very good, sir. Three notes."

I led my half of the cavalry across the span to the Rome side of the river once more, followed by Tullia and Homer. The low ridge there would hide us while we waited. Fortunately there was also a hollow behind it on the left-hand side, deep enough that a rider could crouch in the saddle there and not be seen. But we dismounted, to be safe; and I ordered the men to rub their polished armor with dirt, so that it would not be noticed from a distance. Reluctantly – for they were proud of the shine – they obeyed.

"I could get used to this," I commented to Tullia.

"I can see that," she replied, "from the way you're throwing out your chest. But seriously, Aulus, it's a good plan. I just hope Volturcius comes soon. It's cold." She pulled her cloak tight. Her veil was long since gone.

"By the way," I said, "I am under orders from the Consul to make sure you don't do anything rash. Just leave it to the cavalry this time, will you?"

She started to protest, and then just snorted. "Show some sense, Aulus. Who are you going to leave the negotiating to, Pomptinus? By Hercules, you can hear his snoring from here." And she asked a rider to go over and stop the noise.

Deep night fell, with only a sliver of moon to light the rustling countryside. The dew was heavy, and our cloaks were not much comfort as we lay in the grass. Tullia, Homer, and I nestled at the top of the hollow, peering down the road and listening. Tullia's eyes never left it, and Homer for once was not drowsy, and he quoted no poets. Instead there was a sparkle in his eyes: he was longing for vengeance on Volturcius.

All night long we waited, watching. But we might as well have laid our ambush in the Land of the Dead, for not a living soul appeared on the road. The sliver of moon sank over the horizon, and still we kept our watch. At last, as I felt the dawn breeze flow down the river valley and the eastern sky began to glow, we heard the distant fall of horses' hoofs.

"Can you see anything?" I whispered to Tullia.

"There, sir," said Homer, "I think I see them, look there!"

I followed his pointing finger, and sure enough there was a new shadow on the flat, dark land. Tullia breathed a deep sigh of relief. Soon the shadow grew nearer and we could see distinct figures riding briskly in the growing light – many Celtic warriors, perhaps sixty, the feathers in their helmets waving up and down. They were closing quickly, making for the bridge. There was a large figure in their midst, the Druid by his shape. And next to him rode a man in a white toga, his head concealed in the hood of his black cloak.

I signaled to the riders in the hollow, and they stood to their horses, grasping their spears, but we did not mount up yet, nor make a noise. I clenched my teeth. Would the sergeant on the far bank be ready? Would he cut off their forward escape?

The Celts reached the approach to the bridge. Were they pausing there? No, they were onto it, crossing it. The trumpeter at my side blew three clear notes, shockingly loud after the hours of silence.

"Now, stay back!" I said to Tullia, as we heard shouting on the far bank and the stamping hoofs of the sergeant's force cutting off the enemy's way forward. I threw myself onto the white mare, dug in my heels, and roared over the lip of the hollow, followed by my force of twenty-five.

The enemy had reached the middle of the bridge. The Celtic warriors were packed in tight there, with the Druid in their midst. The sergeant's riders had blocked the far end, spears leveled, and now my own men swung round in perfect formation to prevent a retreat. We had them trapped, but would they fight?

I had to admire the Celts. Not only were they a striking group – each man being dressed as he pleased, and as ferociously as possible – but they also now displayed an iron discipline. They did not scatter, or panic, or even shout out, or show their surprise. At a single word from their captain they lowered their spears and hugged their shields to their bellies.

We sat on our mounts staring at each other. I had stopped my horse in front of our line; and though I could not make out much through the screen of Celts, there seemed to be one point of commotion in their midst. A man was darting around on foot inside the press of horses, dashing from one side of the bridge to the other, letting out panicked shrieks. Otherwise the enemy was silent.

"How is it, sergeant?" I roared.

"All secure, sir," came the faint reply from the other side.

I advanced my horse further, meeting the dull stares of the warriors.

"Volturcius, come out!" I roared again. "We know you're in there! Come out!"

A figure in white peered around the nearest horses, edging inch by inch into view. He had shed his cloak.

"Volturcius," I called, "Volturcius, I arrest you in the name of the Senate and the People of Rome. Come out and you shall be taken to the city."

The horses shifted, and there he stood, framed between two warriors and stricken with amazement.

"It's you!" he cried. "What can this be? The slave – the magician's slave! Impossible!"

"And here is the magician!" said Homer, coming up on the donkey. "But you're mistaken, Volturcius! He is not my slave: he is Aulus Lucinus Spurinna, the nephew of the man you murdered in Etruria!"

"Help me!" cried Volturcius, turning to the Celts, and running to the Druid's horse. "Come on!" he said, grasping at the Druid's leg. "We can break through! Otherwise we're ruined! Charge now, cut our way through!"

I saw the great red beard of the Druid as it advanced toward us, and I recognized the glint in his eye. I had seen it in the alley behind Volturcius' house, when he prayed to his strange gods to destroy me.

But then the strangest thing happened.

I had been so intent on arresting Volturcius that I had not – in spite of Cicero's strict orders – paid any attention when Tullia had ridden up with Homer. Nor had I noticed when she dismounted. Now she flung the reins to Homer and to my horror she rushed towards the Druid. Volturcius shrank back from them, clinging to his horse, for the Druid was suddenly laughing. And now he was dismounting too, his large legs landing smartly on the ground, and he opened his arms to Tullia. She all but sprang into them, and they embraced.

"Does he have the letter?" she asked.

"It's in his saddlebag," came the Druid's sing-song answer. The captain of the Celts reached in to remove it, and handed it to Tullia.

"Here, Aulus, come take this," she called. I dismounted and approached them, as though walking in a dream. "Here it is," she said. "And here is Brennus, if I may introduce him. An Ambassador of the Allobroges, and, as you know, a Druid."

Volturcius' eyes were round as eggs. He stared now at Tullia, now at Brennus. He began to shake, as though he were in the presence of the supernatural at last. But with a cry he slipped away, out of the captain's grip. He rushed to the side of the bridge, hesitated for blink of an eye, and threw himself over the side.

We sprang to the edge ourselves, but his splash was lost in the foam. Was he gone? But then there came another splash, just below us, as another figure leapt into the stream.

"Homer!" I cried.

I stared into the rushing water. Two figures were struggling, carried by the current. Homer's head bobbed up as he thrashed with Volturcius, both gasping for air, but Homer had him by the shirt – and he was not about to let go.

"He'll drown!" I cried, forgetting about Tullia, the Druid, the Celts, and the cavalry. I flew back down the bridge, leaping the last bit of wall, stumbling down the riverbank and then along the shore.

"Homer, where are you? Homer!" I raced up and down the bank; but neither my uncle's murderer nor my uncle's secretary could be seen. I shouted incoherently.

"Over here, down here, sir!" came a faint cry, far down-stream. And there he was in the middle of a reed bed, crawling on his knees and spitting. "Here, sir, over this way!" His right hand grasped at the mud as he pulled himself free of the reeds, onto the bank. His left hand was locked around Volturcius' ankle.

So there they lay as we ran up – Tullia and the Druid with me, and a crowd of Celts and cavalry troopers behind – side by side in the mud, Volturcius sprawling and coughing, Homer dazed but faintly triumphant.

I was speechless. I lifted him up. I slapped him on the back. But no words came. At last I managed to speak. "Homer, I didn't know you could swim!"

"To be honest," he answered weakly, "I didn't know it either, sir. I think we were lucky with the current. But I couldn't let him get away, sir! Not Volturcius!"

We turned to the waiting crowd. They gave him three cheers, echoing across the fields.

The Druid spoke. "You have a remarkable slave, sir," he said to me. "I have never seen anything like it. This jumping into the river. And the performance he gave at Volturcius' house! That was quite . . . what is the word? It was excellent, fantastic."

I stared at him, the full strangeness of it returning to me. "You mean," I said, "you were *with* us the whole time? At that dinner?"

Tullia cut in. "I'm sorry, Aulus, really . . . I didn't mean to trick you, you know, and I'm sorry for it. But you had to see the letter and testify to the Judges, and it was so important that Volturcius should not suspect Brennus. Oh, I've been dying to tell you all about it for the last ten days!"

"But . . . but . . . but you chased me through the house!" I exclaimed. "And down the alley!"

"Oh, Spurinna, I apologize," said the Druid earnestly. "I was trying to give you the letter, you see, but you are such a fast runner and my Latin sometimes fails me." He smiled. "But I admit it may be that I can look frightening. Even your slave here, who I think is not afraid of much in this world, was nervous at that dinner, looking over at me."

"My slave?" I asked. It was all falling into place. Tullia's mysterious evasions, and the chase through the house, and the way the Celts had not seemed surprised on the bridge. "My slave? Yes, a wonderful man," I said. "Quite fearless. But you've reminded me of something, something important."

I took the letter from where it lay in Tullia's open hand, that vital piece of proof; and I put it safely in my toga pouch. But I had two other documents in there already: one was the Judges' letter of protection for my aunt, and the other – well, I took the other one out.

"Homer, dry your hands. And take this." I gave him the third document.

"What's this, sir?"

"Well, Homer, I . . . that is to say, I want you to know that even if we've had our disagreements in backgammon, and so on, and the black sheep, and all that . . . well, I have always thought highly of you. I'm a lucky man to have you, and my uncle would be proud of you today. Very proud, Homer."

"Sir, thank you. But if I may observe, you haven't said what this . . ."

"It's a certificate of freedom. I got the scribes to write it out before we left. I'm freeing you, Homer."

He stared. Now at the certificate, and now again at me. His eyes filled with tears as the men gave him three more cheers, now louder and longer than ever.

"Sir . . . sir!" he stammered. "Sir, I . . . I don't know what to say, sir, for the first time in my life! I haven't felt this happy since . . . since I first read the first line of Hesiod!"

"Hesiod?" the Druid broke in. "Now that you mention it, sir," he said to Homer, "now that you mention it, I have been thinking about your praise of that poet, and what you said at dinner. Afterward it gave me much to reflect upon. Now, sir, I should like to know more about this Hesiod. You do not happen to know something of his actual poetry, do you?"

The Battle for Rome

By now the sun was rising high, reflected in the rushing river; it dried the grass beside the road, and there we lit cooking fires and thought of breakfast. We put Volturcius in chains and Homer seized the chance to deprive him of his toga, wrapping it around himself, for he was now a Roman citizen. It was of the finest cloth, though slightly too small for him.

"You won't need it where you're going," he remarked to our prisoner with a certain glee.

All order in the ranks of cavalry and Celts had disappeared when they had crowded down to watch Homer pull Volturcius from the water. They had witnessed Homer's freedom as a mingled mass of men. But it seemed I was lucky to have such an audience, for as we sat down to eat – neither the cavalry nor the Celts had touched anything since the evening before – they drank my health respectfully but merrily, and all together. Everyone agreed it had been a noble gesture, and though the Celts spoke no Latin and the riders no Celtic, they took turns doing impressions of Homer's reaction. They were hitting it off. For their part, Homer and the Druid were already deep in Hesiod's unfairly neglected minor works.

I had other priorities, naturally. I brought Tullia her toasted bread and demanded an explanation.

"Really, Aulus, it's quite simple," she answered, "I'm surprised you haven't figured it out. Brennus was one of the Celtic Ambassadors, as you know, here about the lawsuit they were pleading. Well, Catiline approached him and promised he would help them in their dispute, if they would help the conspiracy. They were thinking about it, but Brennus judged that Catiline would fail."

"A smart move," I remarked.

"Luckily – for us, at least!" Tullia said. "But he couldn't speak directly to my father, because some of the other Ambassadors were very cautious, and he had doubts about father. And father had doubts about him. We knew all about the letter. Father thought it was a trick, but I believed Brennus was honest. He was the one who convinced the conspirators to write it the letter and to sign it. But then how could we get at it? Once Volturcius had it, he wouldn't even let Brennus touch it. We didn't know when Volturcius would try to deliver it. That's where you came in."

"I see."

"Well, thanks to my plan, and to Fulvia, and to Fulvia's friend, and to your slave, you were able to testify to the Judges, and now you know the rest."

"I still think you could have told me," I said.

"And I still think I couldn't have," she replied, but she smiled.

Soon breakfast ended, and I gave the word to put out the cooking fires and make ready to ride back. As we were packing, however, the Druid shielded his eyes from the sun and gave a cry. "Spurinna! I think there are soldiers moving on the road there. Do you see the dust?"

He was right; but we were still wondering what it could mean when a man rode up at full gallop. He reined in where I was standing with the sergeant and Tullia, and he saluted. I saw he was in uniform.

"Where is Flaccus?" he asked. "I have orders for Flaccus from the Consul Antonius."

The sergeant told him Flaccus had fallen out, and I was now in charge.

"You?" cried the messenger, but the sergeant seemed about to strike him so he added hastily, "Yes, of course. Spurinna from Etruria, you say? Very good. Well, sir, the Consul Antonius is marching today, sir, against Catiline. And we are short of cavalry, sir, so he requests politely that Flaccus and the – that is, that you and the cavalry will join him at the fourth milestone from the city. Immediately, sir."

"We can do that," I said; and raising my voice I addressed the men. "Soldiers, the Consul is marching against the traitor Catiline. We ride to join him. We ride to battle. Are you with me?"

Despite their lack of sleep, they were keen. One anonymous voice called out from the back, "We're with you! We ride with Spurinna!"

I turned to the Druid. "Brennus," I said, "you've heard. Your Celts will have to escort Volturcius back the way you came."

At this the Druid cleared his throat and said, "That would be well. Yet the captain has asked me to tell you, Spurinna, that his warriors would prefer to accompany you to battle. Indeed, they beg you to allow them to come. They are rather fierce," he added quietly, "and they get restless without a battle every few months."

"Do they?" I replied. "Well, let them come. But you're staying?"

"I should return and explain the situation to Cicero," he answered. "We have never trusted one another fully, but this man Homer will come with me, if you allow it. He is known to the Consul, and can produce the letter of proof and describe our good deeds. And perhaps the Consul's daughter will come with us?"

"Brennus, you are not serious!" said Tullia. "I wouldn't miss a battle for the earth!"

Tullia was as sad as I was to see Homer go, riding beside the Druid with Volturcius firmly between them. Homer had given the prisoner his donkey and taken Volturcius' horse in exchange. In one hand he grasped the letter with the conspirators' signatures, and in his new toga pouch lay his certificate. Half a dozen Celtic warriors made up the party.

"See you soon, sir!" cried Homer, turning back. "Half a month at most, I think!"

"Say hello to Pantolemos, won't you?" I called.

"'Say hello? I'm going to rub his nose in it for days!" He smiled as he and the Druid turned round a bend, taking the road to Rome.

For our part, we were ready to ride, and the trumpeter sounded the signal to move out. Though they must have been as tired as I was, the men were in high spirits. It appeared that the five riders whom Flaccus had first put under my command now considered themselves my bodyguard, and they rode beside us. The good feeling between cavalry and Celts continued, I saw, as we made our way in good order toward the fourth milestone. This lay to the south, for the army was not taking the Mulvian Bridge across the river but rather the main bridge, which

Homer and I had crossed on our first day in the city.

Still, it was noon by the time we reached the main body of the army – an amazing number of armed men to see in one place at one time. I had thought our fifty riders and fifty warriors were a strong force; but there were several thousands already in the camp, and more coming up from Rome. Not many riders, however: they were mostly on foot, with spears and shields. Tullia rode off to pay her respects to friends, so I left my troop with the sergeant and went to find the Consul, Antonius.

"You must not refer to Cicero as 'the Consul,'" I reminded myself several times as I approached Antonius' large white tent. "In this army *Antonius* is the Consul, and he's probably jealous of Cicero, so be careful."

"Spurinna?" came a voice from inside, and I straightened my red cloak. But it seemed the voice was not addressing me, though it did belong to Antonius. "Who's this Spurinna? I thought it was going to be young Flaccus. Didn't he command this troop? He's that Judge's nephew, after all."

"Spurinna's from Etruria, sir," said another voice, a staff officer. "He may be useful when we get there. Also, a friend of the other Consul's. Flaccus fell ill yesterday."

"Very well. Go find him."

The staff officer emerged from the tent, an intelligent middle-aged man who clearly knew his duty. I introduced myself, and he showed me in.

"Ah, Spurinna," said Antonius when he saw me. I had expected him to be dressed just like Cicero, but he was in military uniform, a big man sitting on a small stool. I saw he was sizing me up and looking a bit skeptical about my age. "Good to meet you. You're young, eh? But I understand Cicero thinks highly of you."

I agreed modestly, though the fact was that Cicero had not foreseen my leading a hundred cavalry: I had just been sent to protect Tullia. But I did not mention this point.

"Popular man, Cicero," Antonius sniffed. "Nice to have him for a Protector, eh? Myself, I just wanted to reach the Consulship like my father and my grandfather did. Were any of your ancestors ever Consul?" he asked sharply.

"I'm afraid you'll have to wait to ask my grandson that, sir," I replied.

"Will I, now? Well, I'll do that," Antonius answered, somewhat taken aback. "Now, Spurinna, to business. We're marching to deal with this Manlius, and Catiline too, as you know. It's fortunate that we found you, because we're short on cavalry. How many riders have you got?"

"Fifty, sir. But we also picked up fifty Celts on horseback this morning, and they were so keen to join us that I thought it was worth it to double our force."

"Fifty Celts, eh? And can you guarantee their loyalty?"

"Yes, sir. Good fighters, too."

"Yes. So, a hundred. That's good. That's very good. It means a lot in this ramshackle – that is, in this particular army." His opinion of me seemed to be rising: perhaps I was more valuable than I looked. "You shall be the horse reserve, alright? No scouting for you, and you may not see action, but that's what a reserve is for. Just keep up to the headquarters."

"Very good, sir."

The next few days showed that keeping up to the headquarters was no difficult thing. The army was marching into Etruria, taking the same road Homer and I had followed a month before on our way to Rome. But what had taken us five days in the rain now took fifteen. Antonius had three legions, hastily raised by himself and Cicero when it was decided to carry the war to Manlius. They were men from the city, mostly, without experience. The veteran legions had been recalled from the East, but it could take months for them to reach Italy.

Furthermore, we had different reports about where Manlius and Catiline now were. At first we thought they were staying in Etruria, but then the scouts said they were making straight for Rome, and we spent two days getting into a defensive position near Lake Volsinium, just by the inn where the young man tried to take my wallet. Then they said this was wrong, and Manlius was moving north – he had reached the border of Gaul, they said, but had run into the Roman army there and had doubled back, returning to Etruria. In any case we kept marching north, though my own troop did not have much to do. The December rain soaked us night after night.

I had not seen Antonius in seven days when he summoned me, after a long march, to the Consul's tent one evening. The sun was dropping to the horizon, but from the knoll where the tent was pitched I could see that we were not very far from my own valley; we had passed through Faesulae that morning. I had ridden in to see my old school, but the whole town was deserted. Perhaps that was for the best. In my cavalry uniform I didn't look much like the student I had been only months before, whose grasp of Greek grammar had always made my teacher frown. And the teacher might have started begging this fierce young officer to spare the building and the scrolls, which would have been very embarrassing.

"Ah yes, young Spurinna," said Antonius when I entered his tent. He looked more tired now as he sat behind a makeshift desk, which was covered with maps. "How are you? A cup of wine, there, for this young man. And for me." He stared at the maps and frowned. "I understand you're from Etruria, Spurinna."

"I am, sir. I grew up not very far from these parts, two miles north. My house is there."

"Just so, just so. Well, come with me."

Antonius rose heavily and pushed me gently out the flap of the tent, leading me to the top of the high ground.

"You may not realize it, young man, but Manlius' army is in front of us, and we know that Catiline is with him!" Antonius' eyes shone as he conveyed this information; it was plain that he wanted to defeat them and share some of Cicero's glory.

"Where, sir?" I asked.

"On the far side of this valley, in the woods. You'll see the fires when it gets dark. I'm giving the men a chance to rest from the march tonight, but tomorrow we fight!" He savored the idea for a moment, and then pointed down the valley. "I want to ask you about the river there," he began.

"River?" I said, following his finger. "Oh, sir, it's no river, except in the spring. Nothing but a stream, if that, at this time of year. That's just the light glinting."

"So men could cross it? In armor?"

I assured him they would have no trouble.

"Good," he said. "Now the next thing. The ridge behind them. Do you see the one I mean?"

"Yes, sir. Around here we call it the Crow's Drop."

"Indeed? And can they cross it? You see it's just behind them. Would it block Manlius' retreat?"

"It would block it, sir, unless they had ropes for every man, or they knew how to climb pretty well."

"Better and better," said Antonius. "Now they just have the road to fall back on, where it winds south there to the left. Thank you, Spurinna. Now, another cup?"

I thanked him, but asked if I might have no more for now. I also asked if there was any chance of a battle tonight.

"Tonight? In the dark? Quite impossible," he chuckled. "It would be chaos. Set your mind at ease about that. But come dawn," he said, looking serious, "come dawn, we fight."

I made my way back to my troop, where the sergeant already had them cooking their dinner. The Celts were positively celebrating, for news was spreading that Manlius was near. Their captain gave me a low bow, said something in Celtic, and shook his spear. I grinned and nodded.

Tullia was sitting off by herself, wrapped in her cloak against the wind.

"Hello there," I said, "I just spoke with Antonius. There's going to be a battle tomorrow."

"So I heard," she said. "And I'm happy to hear it. This marching back and forth day after day gets very boring."

"Would you like to march a bit more tonight?" I asked. "I'm going to go pay a visit up in the valley. It's not that far a ride, though we have until dawn. My house is there."

"Your house? I had no idea we were near it. Of course I'd like to see your house, Aulus," she said, springing up and running for her saddle. My unofficial bodyguard had overheard us, and they too hurried for their horses.

"It's not much," I insisted, as we left the camp and trotted up the lane of cypress I knew so well. "Just an ordinary place with farms, you know. A bit old-fashioned."

"I'm sure it's paved with old Roman virtues," Tullia answered. "You're far too modest, Aulus."

Dusk was falling. But I was surprised, as we rode onto our land and began to pass the tenants' cottages, to notice there were no lights flickering in the windows. The fields looked untidy, as though they had been harvested very hastily; and we saw no farmers standing in the common vegetable plot, gossiping as they liked to do in the evening. The land looked deserted.

We reached the front of the lane that led to our house. There was no one at the gate. But we did see a candle flickering in the slaves' quarters, and in the air was a faint smell of beans baking. I dismounted, leaving Tullia and the horsemen in the courtyard, and walked up to see what was going on.

"Who is it?" came a rough voice from inside, in answer to my knock.

"It's me, Aulus!" I called. "Open up, will you?"

The door was swung open, slowly and cautiously. Inside I saw one of our tenants eyeing me with mistrust, a lighted lamp in one hand and his pitchfork in the other.

"Why, so it is!" he exclaimed, lowering the sharp prongs. "It's Master Aulus, back from Rome! Call the mistress, girl! It's Master Aulus!"

I stepped inside, as lamps appeared in the doorways. The hall was full of people, mostly women from the farms, all staring at me with open-mouthed surprise.

And soon there came a clatter of feet, and Aunt Hercna herself was there in the kitchen doorway.

"Aulus!" she cried, rushing up and throwing her arms around me. "You're back! I can't believe it! Where have you been?"

We held each other's arms, and stared at each other. She seemed older than before my uncle died, as though she had aged far more than a month while I'd been gone. Her voice had a rasp to it that I did not recognize.

"Yes, it's me!" I said, and we laughed. "But tell me, what's going on here? No lights at the farmers' places, and a pitch-fork welcome at the door! Is it a plague?"

My aunt didn't answer at first, but led me to a chair and sat opposite. Then she told me everything: how Manlius had become more aggressive after I left, insulting her openly, and laughing at her threats. It seemed he had a lot more men now, and the farmers didn't dare say anything – *she* didn't dare, even – when they appeared as the harvest was ready and took all the grain. "To feed that big camp he's got, Aulus," she said with a mixture of sadness and anger. "And they took everything – even the barley! He stripped the fields!" The farmers had fled to the house, which Manlius had not dared to attack just yet; but why would he even bother? They had been left there to starve, no threat to his plans for now.

"But did you see him?" my aunt asked at last. "Did you see the Consul Cicero? After you left, I said to myself: It's no use to have sent a boy off like that, it's hopeless to think the Consul of Rome . . . I should never have let you go, Aulus. But why were you gone so long? We were sure you were dead, killed on that dangerous road to the city."

"I'm alive," I confirmed with a smile.

"And where is Homer?" she continued. "Did he bother you much? You haven't lost him, have you?"

"No, no," I said. "I sent him off. I freed him."

"Freed him?" she cried. "Oh, but, Aulus, how could you do that? Think of the money! We can't afford to free a valuable slave like Homer. How will we pay for your school now? Oh, if only your uncle. . ." She began to weep quietly.

Just then a man rushed in, one of the household slaves.

"They're here!" he cried. "Manlius is here! Not many with him, but they're on horses and they've got spears! Six of them, in the courtyard!"

Suddenly real panic gripped the hall, and a lamp smashed on the floor as people hurried to gather their families.

"No, no!" I exclaimed. "Be calm, please! Listen now, it's not Manlius, it's just my bodyguard. I'll go get them."

"Your bodyguard?" said my aunt, looking up from her chair.

"Yes, here they are," I continued, as the men walked in, followed by Tullia. "Look, it's not Manlius at all, it's me." The men saluted my aunt, and Tullia waved politely.

"Aulus," said my Aunt, "have you gone and joined the cavalry?"

"No, I haven't. It's just temporary. We're here with the army, with Antonius."

"Aulus is commanding the cavalry reserve, madam," put in Tullia.

"The cavalry reserve . . . ? Commanding . . . ? I don't understand," said Aunt Herena. "You'll have to explain. Sit down again. And who is this young lady?" she asked, indicating Tullia.

"Oh, this is Tullia. She's the Consul's daughter, and we couldn't get rid of her. Say hello, Tullia."

"The Consul's daughter!" my aunt nearly shrieked. "Good heavens, forgive me, please, please sit down here. I had no idea. Aulus, really, how can this be?" Poor Aunt Hercna was gravely flustered, pained perhaps at the lack of food fit to offer a guest, and she began summoning the cook and servants.

"No, really, madam," objected Tullia, "it's fine. We ate in the camp. Please don't fuss. Besides, I really am looking forward to watching Aulus explain what he's been up to."

At last all three of us took a seat, while half a dozen farming families eavesdropped openly. I took it from the first night at the roadside inn all the way to the arrest of Volturcius at the Mulvian Bridge. And all the while my aunt's shock gave way to a sort of speechless amazement.

She patted her cheek as each new adventure was described, exclaiming, "You, Aulus, and the Consul!" or, "You, Aulus, and the Judges!" or just a simple, "You, Aulus! You!" which made Tullia laugh rather too much, I thought. But I could see the old pride rising in Aunt Hercna's eye, the old fire, and by the time I got to the part about the bridge, she looked just like my old aunt again. I didn't mention that my uncle had really been murdered, for Homer and I had taken care of that anyway.

"And it was Cicero's own scribes who wrote out Homer's certificate," I finished. "Oh, and also I forgot to mention this."

I produced the magnificent papyrus document that the Judges had signed. Aunt Hercna took it without a word and read it to herself.

"'. . . guarantees the right of Spurinna and his Tenants to their land, and also the Protection, the special Protection of that right, from the Senate and the Roman People . . .'" she read in a whisper. And then she read it again. And when she looked up she was crying, my dear old stern Roman lady of an aunt, crying in front of the tenants.

"You did it, Aulus," she whispered. "I don't know how! My nephew!"

And with uncharacteristic generosity she ordered ten jars of wine to be opened for the farmers, and all the candles to be lit, and she herself led me by the hand to the old shrine of the household gods where I had performed the offering when my uncle died. Still crying, she said a prayer of thanks. The tenants greeted me again, with no hesitation this time, as "Aulus Lucinus Spurinna, keeper of the peace, Protector of the valley, upholder of the Law!" That dried my aunt's tears; she was beaming.

"Now," she said, turning to me, "if only if it weren't for that Manlius, our troubles would all be over. Shouldn't you be going?"

"Going?" I asked, taken aback.

"You said you came with the army," Aunt Hercna answered, "and everyone in the valley knows there's going to be a battle tomorrow. Shouldn't you be getting back? Aren't you commanding the cavalry reserve?"

I left Tullia at the house, talking the latest fashion in Rome with my aunt and eating a big plate – she couldn't refuse twice – of baked beans. I would never have guessed Aunt Hercna cared at all for such things, but there she was, already learning a lot about the latest silk dresses, interspersed with political ideas, as I left with the riders. I took my own javelins from out back, glad to have them with me again.

"Is it your house that I see, sir?" asked one of my bodyguards as we rode down the lane.

"Yes."

"And a fine place," he said sincerely. "I do prefer the old style myself. But I'm sorry that Tullia, that is to say, the Consul's daughter, is staying and missing the fight. I wouldn't be surprised one bit if she knew how to charge with a spear. I mean, the lady knows how to ride, sir!"

But his regrets were premature, and in fact no one was surprised when Tullia rejoined us the next morning. But for once she promised to stay away from the battle. Only, she added, because Antonius needed company, and generals usually had the best view of the action.

"But I shall be watching your troop, Aulus," she did say. "So don't find yourself attacking the wrong people or I shall tell my father all about it."

The Consul joined us. "Ah, Tullia," he said. "I'm glad you're here. Now the whole city will hear about our victory as soon as possible." He turned to me. "Good weather for a battle, eh? But my orders for you, Spurinna, are to hold back from the first assault here by the Praetorian Guard. Manlius is coming down now, and we must see what develops. But be ready to move at a moment's notice."

It was a bright, cold morning. We extinguished the cooking fires and mounted up, but little was happening. The sergeant offered me a big cup of hot wine, which I sipped as I gazed across at Manlius' force: it looked like four legions, a trifle smaller than ours, standing in ranks not half a mile away.

"Sergeant," I asked him, "I don't understand why they're just standing there. Don't they see we're going to beat them?"

He smiled grimly and said, "Well, sir, as to that, two reasons spring to mind. The first is that they can't run, not with the Campanian legion sitting on the south road to the left there. And the second is, I think they plan to beat *us*."

"The Consul Antonius seemed confident," I observed.

"Yes, sir," said the sergeant. "Which is why I'm not the Consul."

Now trumpets on both sides sounded, all down the long lines of foot soldiers, a grim symphony. But still no one moved.

"They're waiting for the skirmishers, sir, the slingers," my sergeant said.

And sure enough I could just see lone figures picking their way through the fields, and I heard the dim whistle of the slings sending deadly stones among both armies. They were like two thin clouds, converging. When they met, we heard faint cries, and it appeared our own slingers were being driven back.

Now the right flank of Manlius' army advanced on our left flank, where the Campanian legion waited on the south road. I saw a figure in front of the enemy lines there, making a speech we could not hear.

"That'll be Manlius himself," said the sergeant. "Tough old dog. I served under him out East, back in the old days."

After his speech, Manlius raised his sword. He led his troops against the Campanians, and soon the ringing and clanking of battle reached us. At about the same time we heard reports that our right flank, over behind the trees, was under assault and being driven back.

"Where are our orders?" I wondered aloud. I could see Manlius making great progress now, though nothing was happening in the center. There both sides' skirmishers were still fighting.

Soon word came that our right flank had not broken: it was holding out in the woods, defending the end of the line. Fighting now began in the center, where both lines pressed against each other, hoping by sheer weight to push the enemy back. But the Campanians on the left were breaking, dozens of men running back, and the rest being slowly encircled by Manlius' old soldiers. We could hear the enemy legions singing.

A rider galloped up from the Consul, ordering us to move to the left and watch the slope, keeping in plain view to encourage the men. I said good-bye to Tullia and off we rode.

Reaching our new position, I had a clearer view of what was happening. Manlius simply had more men, and you could see him not far below, riding to and fro with his bodyguard. The Campanians were reforming, but it looked like time was running out.

"There they go, sir!" said the sergeant, pointing to the center. From the point we had just left, the Praetorian Guard was marching down the slope toward the heart of the battle. They were easy to spot: the only forces on either side with a real uniform, and they knew how to march in step. They locked their shields together, chanting like a single man with a giant voice. And then they charged.

Actually, you can't really charge with a shield that size, in full armor; but they managed to jog, and the worn-out legion in front of them made way as they slammed against the enemy center. It was like a wave of steel roaring against the beach. The enemy was falling back – no, they were running.

"The center! The center gives way!" came the cry.

But now the enemy center stopped running and began to rally. A splendid figure in golden armor had appeared in their midst. He dashed to and fro, trying to bring them back to the fight, and at last his trumpets sounded and he threw himself into the Praetorians like a lightning bolt.

"Catiline! Catiline rides!" came the cry from below, and all Manlius' forces stopped to try and watch.

But the Praetorians held. Their ranks shuddered, and you could trace the golden figure's path through them as he and his bodyguard kept on. But in the end the Praetorians were ranked too deep, and the lightning bolt's progress slowed and stopped at last.

All eyes strained to see, but as usual in battle it was word of mouth that told us of the victory.

"Catiline is down! Catiline has fallen! Catiline has fallen!"

You could hear the celebration of the Praetorians a mile off. And Manlius' troops reacted also. Despite the pleas of their officers, they began to fall back. Many threw away their shields and ran. The line of the enemy center collapsed, and it was plain that our legion on the right was leaving the woods, driving the enemy back and dispersing them like autumn leaves.

Below us, even Manlius could not keep them together, and Catiline's right flank began to melt. But they had the south road open for their escape, for the Campanians were too tired to prevent them.

"Sergeant," I said, "get the men ready. We're moving out. We're going to block that road. Are the Celts ready? Alright now, tell the trumpeter to be prepared."

I put on my helmet and seized my javelin from the ground. The riders around me readied their spears, showing huge relief that they would not be left out of the battle after all. We had received no orders, but I was sure this was right. We would cut off Manlius' escape.

Down the slope now, in good order, getting a cheer from the Campanians as we formed triple ranks, thirty men by three. I had my eye on a wide open stretch of the road to the south, which it seemed that Manlius was making for. We veered off, racing him to it at a brisk trot.

Manlius saw us coming, and he rushed to defend the road, to reach the open stretch before we got there and so to keep the road free. It was the only escape his army had left. I heard him bawling now, calling to his best old soldiers to hurry.

But it was no race at all. We had fine, well-rested horses; his men were tired with battle. We arrived with time to spare, though not much. And it struck me what a fine footing the road made for our horses.

"Well done, sergeant," I said. "But we are not waiting here. Do you see Manlius up in front of us? Well, we're going to charge. Alert the Celtic captain and tell the trumpeter. Watch for my javelin, I'm going to shake it in the air, and then we charge!"

"Very good, sir."

As one man, the Romans leveled their spears; as fifty men, the Celts swung their swords above their heads, each calling out to the Celtic gods for victory. And then I raised my javelin and shook it, and the trumpeter's clear note echoed across the broken battlefield.

We began at a walk, and soon the trot, and then a swift canter. Ahead, Manlius was trying to get his men into ranks, but it was too late. I shook my javelin once more and we reached a full gallop, dashing through Manlius' bodyguard with the fury of the hot south wind. Time seemed to slow down. My bodyguard and I were at the heart of the troop – I couldn't ride as fast as the cavalry – so I didn't see the first clash, but after a blink of an eye I was in among them too, my horse flying straight through two men and on, on over the standard-bearer, on through the second line of spears. Two of my bodyguard fell, one with a spear in his side and the other when his horse tumbled; but I was not hurt. The Celts on our right were making fearful havoc, shouting with each kill. It seemed forever that we

were in among them, stabbing with our spears; but I called
a halt after a hundred yards.

"Where are you, sergeant?"

"Here, sir," he said, riding up. His wrist had been badly
twisted.

"Tell them to form ranks immediately. And tell me, did
we break them?"

"They're broken, sir. The road's ours."

"Then get the men in line across it. Tell them to keep
their spears up, so that the rest can see there's no escape
this way."

"Very good, sir."

While they were gathering, I rode back the way we'd
come. I saw the standard-bearer lying there with a spear
stuck through him, and Manlius' old soldiers were heaped
around, groaning and begging for help. And over in the
ditch, still crawling, I saw the man himself. He had been terribly trampled in the charge, and he was covered in blood.

"Manlius," I began. But I fell silent. There was nothing
to say; he could not recognize me, and I could not explain.
As I watched, he ceased his crawling, gave a final soft sigh,
and died.

So that was the last chapter of the Roman conspiracy, as I
saw it. My family's land was saved forever, my Aunt Hercna
was restored as the lady busy running it, and last year
the tenants held a festival to celebrate the anniversary of

my return, and the battle. Catiline fell fighting, as I've described, at the front of his troops: he got some of the glory he had dreamed of, for everyone agreed it was a brave thing to attack the Praetorians single-handed, but everyone was also glad it was the last glory he would get. I don't think anyone missed Manlius, but it was heart-wrenching to walk the battlefield the next day and see so many Romans killed by other Romans, on both sides. I saw how horrible war could be then, but I couldn't object to the congratulations that Antonius offered me in his victory speech, and the pure joy of my troop was a moving sight to see.

Tullia, too, was pleased, though she joked about my leading a charge without orders. I'm glad to be living in Rome now, for I get to see her quite often, and she takes me to hear the debates and the court cases and generally keeps me up to date on politics. But she thinks I should go out to the East and make a fortune, and she says I should take Homer along. But how can I do that, when he's busy copying this story on papyrus? Sometimes I don't follow Tullia's logic. Cicero's career continues, naturally, with its ups and downs; and as for Julius Caesar – well, that is another story altogether, for another time.

Acknowledgments

I would like to thank my family, first of all, and particularly my brother David, with whom I discussed the plot of this book in detail one afternoon in the Jardin des Plantes in Paris. Kathy Lowinger of Tundra Books placed a great deal of faith in me as an author, for which I am altogether grateful; she and Carolyn Jackson have been invaluable in working out the story and the text. Likewise my thanks go out to Catherine Mitchell, Alison Morgan, Pamela Osti, Kong Njo, and Cindy Reichle at Tundra. And I cannot fail to mention the inspiration of my friendships with Andy and Moira Johnson, Chris Thompson, Dustin Bermudez, Doug Taylor, Wade Richardson, Alessandro Barchiesi, and Richard Martin, and with my many colleagues at Stanford.